SNOWBOUND
BRIDE-TO-BE

SNOWBOUND BRIDE-TO-BE

BY
CARA COLTER

First published in Great Britain 2009
Large Print edition 2010
Harlequin Mills & Boon Limited,
Eton House, 18-24 Paradise Road,
Richmond, Surrey TW9 1SR

© Cara Colter 2009

ISBN: 978 0 263 21203 7

Harlequin Mills & Boon policy is to use papers that are
natural, renewable and recyclable products and made
from wood grown in sustainable forests. The logging and
manufacturing process conform to the legal environmental
regulations of the country of origin.

Printed and bound in Great Britain
by CPI Antony Rowe, Chippenham, Wiltshire

To Alice Sonntag,
who gave me a Christmas wreath
with the word *believe*
peeking out of fragrant boughs.

CHAPTER ONE

TWENTY-TWO gallons of hot chocolate.

Ten of mulled wine.

Four hundred and sixty-two painstakingly decorated Christmas cookies.

And no one was coming.

The storm battering the windows of the White Pond Inn—Emma White had rechristened it the White Christmas Inn just this morning—was being compared by the radio announcer to the Great Ice Storm of 1998 that had wreaked havoc on this region of Atlantic Canada, not to mention Quebec, Ontario, New York and New England.

Christmas was clearly going to be ruined.

"Just like always," Emma murmured out loud to herself, her voice seeming to echo through the empty inn.

Her optimism was not in the least bolstered by

the fire crackling cheerfully in the hearth, by her exquisite up-country holiday decorations in the great room, or by her bright-red Santa hat and her lovely red wool sweater with the white angora snowflakes on its front.

In fact, speaking the thought out loud—that Christmas was going to be ruined, just like always—invited a little girl, the ghost of herself, to join her in the room.

The little girl had long, dark wavy hair and was staring at an opened package that held a doll with jaggedly cut hair and blue ink stains on its face, clearly not Clara, the doll she had whispered to Santa that she coveted, but rather a cast-off of one of the children her mother cleaned houses for.

"Shut up," Emma ordered herself, but for some reason the little ghost girl wanted her to remember how she had pretended to be happy. For her mother.

Her mother, Lynelle, who had finally agreed to come for Christmas. Emma could not wait to show her the refurbished house that Lynelle had grown up in but not returned to since she was sixteen, not even when Grandma had died.

Emma tried not to think that her mother had sounded backed into a corner rather than enthused about spending Christmas here. And she had agreed to come only on Christmas Eve, taking a miss on the seasonal celebrations at the inn: the ten-day pre-Christmas celebration, Holiday Happenings. But still Lynelle would be here for the culmination of all Emma's hard work and planning, Christmas Day Dream.

Lynelle's lack of enthusiasm probably meant she was distracted. In Emma's experience that usually meant a new man.

It was probably uncharitable—and unChristmas-like—but when Emma sent the bus ticket, she was sending fare for a single passenger.

The radio cut into her thoughts, but only to add to her sense of unease and gloom. "This just in, the highway closed at Harvey all the way through to the U.S. border."

Emma got up and deliberately snapped off the radio, thoughts of her mother and her memories. She tried to focus on the facts, to be pragmatic, though the inn was plenty of evidence that prag-matism did not come naturally to her. The inn was the project of a dreamer, not a realist.

Okay, she told herself, visitors would not be making the scenic drive up from Maine tonight. Maybe it was just as well. Her aging neighbor, Tim Fenshaw, had already called to say he couldn't bring the horses out in this, so there would be no sleigh rides. The phone line had gone dead before he had said good-bye.

And just before the last light had died in the evening sky, Emma had looked out her back window at her pond and seen that it was being covered with snow faster than she could hope to clear it. So, no skating, either.

"Holiday Happenings is not happening," Emma announced to herself. Or at least not happening tonight, which was to have been the opening night of ten days of skating and sleigh rides right up until Christmas Eve.

It was all adding up to a big fat zero. No sledding, no sleigh rides, no skating, no admission fees, no hot dog sales, no craft sales, no cookie sales. All the things Emma had counted on *finally* to bring the inn firmly into the black.

And to finance her Christmas Day Dream.

"Would one little miracle be so much to ask

for?" she asked out loud, sending an irritated look heavenward.

The Christmas Day Dream was Emma's plan to provide a very special Christmas for those who did not have fantasy Christmases. The disappointments of her childhood had not all occurred at Christmas. But somehow, at that time of year in particular, she had waited for the miracle that didn't come.

Last year she'd thought she had left all of that behind her. She was an adult now, and she had looked forward, finally, to the best Christmas of all. Her then fiancé, Dr. Peter Henderson, had invited her to spend Christmas with his family. The very memory tasted of bitterness. Was it possible last year had been worse than all the rest combined?

Emma had learned her lesson! She was not putting her expectations in the hands of others, not her mother, and not a man!

This year she was in charge. She was devoted to eradicating Christmas disappointments. She was determined to make Christmas joyous, not just for herself, but for a world she knew from personal experience was grimly in need of a dose of true Christmas spirit.

In collusion with several area churches and a homeless shelter, a dozen of the neediest families in this region had received invitations to spend Christmas Day at the inn.

The invitations targeted families with nothing to hope for, families who could not have Christmas, or could not have it as they dreamed it should be.

On Christmas Day Emma was throwing open the doors to fifty-one confirmed guests who would arrive on a chartered bus.

Emma *knew* the people coming: the oldest a seventy-six-year-old grandmother who was the sole guardian of her three grandchildren, one of whom was the youngest, a nine-month-old baby whose two siblings were under age five. The largest group was a family of eight whose father had been hurt in an accident early last year, and had not been able to work since; the smallest was a single mother and her handicapped son.

And, of course, her mother, who understood Christmases with nothing—one year they had not even had a tree—would be there to share in the joy. There would be gifts for everyone. Brand-new. No hairless ink-stained dolls. But more than gifts, the *feeling* would be there. Emma had been collecting skates, and having them sharpened in anticipation of skating, Tim was hooking up the Clydes to give sleigh rides.

His daughter-in-law, Mona, and two granddaughters, Sue and Peggy, who were staying with him while Tim, Jr., served with the Canadian Armed Forces overseas, had practically been living here preparing for Holiday Happenings and the Christmas Day Dream.

Not even last year, anticipating Christmas with the Hendersons, had filled Emma with this sense that by giving this gift to others, she would know the secret of the season, would share in its universal peace.

Now, her dreams felt precarious. *Naive.* She could hear Peter's voice as if he stood next to her.

"How am I going to pay for everything?" she whispered. How was she going to pay the Fenshaws for all the time they had given her? And, indeed, for Christmas Day Dream? And the stacks of wonderful brand-new gifts she'd been foolish enough to put on credit, her optimism had been so high? She hadn't been able to see how Holiday Happenings could possibly fail. She'd been having a dozen calls a day about it since she'd put the posters up in mid-November.

The St. Martin's Church youth group had sent her the admissions in full for thirty-two kids— who were supposed to come tonight. She remembered how gleeful she had been when she had used their money to make a deposit on the chartered bus for her Christmas-Day guests.

Emma could feel a familiar headache pulling between her eyebrows, knotting above the bridge of her nose.

She'd inherited White Pond, the neglected house and overgrown eighteen acres from her grandmother last spring. It had quickly become apparent to her she couldn't afford to keep it.

By then Emma was committed to keeping it. There was something here of her family and her history that Lynelle had scorned, but that Emma *needed*. So, she'd used her life savings, not huge on her wage as a medical reception-ist, given permanent notice to the job she had taken temporary leave from, and risked her engagement, which had already been on the rocks since last Christmas, and which had well and truly washed up on shore when she'd made the decision to come home and care for the grandmother who had been a virtual stranger to her.

And then on a shoe-string budget, with endless determination and elbow grease, Emma had done her best to refurbish the house. She had opened as a bed and breakfast last summer.

It had soon been woefully obvious to her that the B and B business was as tricky and as full of pitfalls as her old house. Still, she had hoped to repair all the foibles of her first summer season with Holiday Happenings.

Again, Emma could sense her former fiancé and boss, Dr. Peter Henderson, his thin face puckered with disapproval, his arms folded over the narrowness of his chest. "Emma," he was saying, "you don't have any idea what you are getting into."

She hated it that with each passing day, his predictions of doom and gloom seemed to be just a little closer to coming true.

And if I had known the full extent of what I was

getting into, would I have— She wasn't allowing herself to think like that.

Emma turned an eye to the inn's tree, a Fraser fir, magnificent in completely white ribbons and ornaments and lights, the angel's wings brushing the ten-foot ceiling. Emma let her eyes rest on that angel for a moment.

"One miracle," Emma said quietly. "I wanted a perfect Christmas. I wanted to give the best gift of all, hope."

The angel gazed back at her with absolute serenity.

"Oh," Emma said, annoyed, "you aren't even a real angel. If I had glass eyes, and paper wings I could look serene, too!"

But then she cast her gaze around the room and her heart softened. The great room of the White Pond Inn had been turned into a picture out of a Christmas fairy tale. This scene was the payoff for all her hard work, and worth the crush of bills, the exhaustion that had become her constant companion.

A fire roared and crackled in the river-rock hearth, colorful woolen socks hung at the solid-slab oak mantle. Garlands of real holly were tacked to crown molding. White poinsettias shone like lights in the dark corners of the room.

Parcels wrapped in shades of white and festooned with homemade bows, containing brand-new dolls and fire trucks were already piled high under that tree, though she had to admit they didn't look quite as pretty when she wasn't sure how she was going to pay for them!

She forced her mind away from that, and finished her inventory of the room. Red-and-white cushions had replaced the ordinary ones on the sofas and chairs, vases held candy canes, the glowing dark planks of the hardwood floors were covered with white area rugs.

The room held a delicious aroma because of the continuous baking that had been happening in the house. The sweet comforting scents of cinnamon and nutmeg and pumpkin and apples had mixed with the smell of the occasional back puff of wood smoke to create a scent that could have been labeled and sold, *Christmas*.

Another great money-making idea from Emma White, she told herself sarcastically, but then she sighed, unable not to enjoy the pleasure of what she had done.

The inn was a vision of Christmas. It was going to bring great joy to many people. When her mother saw it, it would erase every bad Christmas they had ever spent together.

"Holiday Happenings and the Christmas Day Dream will still happen," Emma told herself stubbornly, but details from the ice storm of 1998 insisted on crowding into her head.

The six-day storm had caused billions of dollars in damage, left millions of people without power for periods that had varied from days to weeks. Roads had been closed, trees destroyed, power lines had snapped under the weight of rain turning to ice.

"I could not be so unlucky to have a six-day storm shut down Holiday Happenings completely," she muttered, but then she whispered, "Could I?"

The storm threw shards of ice up against her window and howled under her eaves in answer.

And then, above the howl of the wind, her doorbell chimed its one clanging, broken note, but still an answer to her question about her luck!

Emma's eyes flew to her grandfather clock.

Eight o'clock! Just when people were supposed to arrive. They had come anyway! The miracle had happened! How was it she had not heard cars, slamming doors, voices?

She tried to rein in her happiness. Of course, it could just be Tim, checking to make sure she was all right in the storm.

The Fenshaws had invited her into the fold of this lovely small community as if she belonged here, as if she was one of them. Tim had been interested in the White Pond property for his son when he returned from overseas, but when Emma had told him she had decided to keep it, he and his daughter-in-law Mona had seemed genuinely pleased, as if they had waited all their lives for her to come home to them.

Now, what if she couldn't pay them after the hours and hours they had devoted to making her dreams become a reality? She couldn't have operated the inn for one day without their constant help and support.

A shiver went down her spine. Worse, what if all these dreams, her foolishness as Peter had called it, cost her the inn?

She went and opened the door, and despite the

rush of ice-cold air, her heart beat hopefully in anticipation of guests, maybe locals from Willowbrook who had braved the weather.

Only it wasn't locals.

And it wasn't Tim.

A stranger stood there, the glow from the string of white Christmas lights that illuminated the porch nearly totally blocked by his size. He was tall and impossibly broad across the shoulders. The sense of darkness was intensified by the absolute black of a knee-length wool coat, black gloves, dark, glossy hair, shot through with snowflakes.

His features were shadowed, but even so, Emma could see the perfect cast of his nose, the thrust of high cheekbones, the strength in the jut of his chin.

The stranger was astonishingly, heart-stoppingly handsome, even though the set of his firm mouth was grim, and his eyes were dark, intense and totally forbidding.

Emma shivered under his scrutiny, felt the sweep of his cool gaze take her in from red socks to ridiculous hat, and saw his mouth tighten into an even grimmer line.

It felt to Emma as if the devil himself had decided to pay her an early Christmas visit. In an instant she went from being an independent woman, operating her own business, to one who wished she could strip off her shapeless sweater and the added bulk of the long johns she had put on earlier in preparation for skating and sleigh-riding.

She became a woman who would have given up just about anything to take back the recent disastrous haircut. In an effort to make her life simpler—or maybe to assert it was *her* life—she had cut her long glossy black hair, one of the few things about her that Peter had approved of. In rebellion, set free, heavy waves had turned to impossible, crazy curls. At least the Santa hat would be hiding the worst of it, though Emma wished she wasn't wearing that, too.

There was something alarmingly intriguing in the to-die-for features of the stranger who blocked the light from her front door. As her eyes adjusted to the deep shadow around him, she drank in his features and the expression on his face.

The man looked as if he might have laughed

once, but did no more. He was one of those men who was a puzzle that begged to be solved. Despite the remoteness in him—or maybe deepened because of it—he was temptation personified.

But not to her, a woman sworn to put all her passion into her business and the coming Christmas. A woman who had sworn that the White Pond Inn was going to be *enough* for her, who could not trust herself to make a good decision about men if her life depended on it. No one, after all, had *looked* like a better bet than Peter.

Her intriguing visitor's eyes moved from her to the wreath on her door, taking in the sprigs of white pine interlaced with balsam and grand fir, taking in the gypsophila and tiny white bells, the glory of the homemade white satin bow. Finally, his gaze paused on the little wooden letters, red, inserted in the wreath, peeking out from under a sprig of feathery cedar.

Believe.

His expression hardened and his gaze strayed to the rest of her porch, glancing off the holly wound through the spindles, the red rag rugs, the planters filled with spruce boughs and red berries.

If she was not mistaken, it was contempt that darkened his eyes to pitch before they returned to her face.

Slam the door, she instructed herself. *Whatever he has come here for, you don't have it. And he doesn't have one thing you need, either.*

She reminded herself, sternly, of rule one: independence! Emma already knew, many thanks to her mother—a lesson reinforced by the good doctor—that a man was the easiest way to lose that sense of independence, that sense of owning your own life.

But the weather was providing a cruel reminder that she did not always make the rules for her life. Now she was given another such reminder.

Because, in a breath, closing the door on him was no longer an option. A tiny whimper drew her attention, finally, from the mesmerizing black ice of his eyes.

She was astonished to see that nestled into the huge expanse of his shoulder, made almost invisible by utter stillness and a black blanket that matched his coat, was a baby.

It turned its face from his shoulder, and gazed

at Emma with huge blue eyes, a living version of a doll she had wrapped earlier. The eyes that gazed at her with such solemn curiosity were as innocent as his were world-weary.

A girl, if the bonnet, a strangely lopsided concoction of dark wool, was any indication. Emma realized the hat was on the wrong way.

Despite the fact the visitor who had emerged from the storm looked so formidable, and so without humor, she almost smiled at the backwards hat.

But his words stole the smile and her breath.

"We need a place to stay."

Her mouth moved in protest but not a single, solitary sound emerged from it. Him? Stay here? With all his attractions and mysteries being doubled by his protective stance with the beautiful baby?

"The highway patrol just told me to get off the road. It was going to close behind me."

Say something, she ordered herself, but no sound came out of her mouth.

"Hopefully," he said, "it will just be for a few hours. Until the roads reopen."

Impossible to say yes to him. Even his voice

was dangerous—as unconsciously sensuous as melted chocolate clinging to a fresh strawberry. He was dangerous to a woman like her who had made vows about the course her life was now going to take. *No more begging for approval, married to the inn.* And yet here she was, wanting to snatch the Santa hat off her head *for him.*

So, impossible to say yes. And even more impossible to say no.

He had a baby with him.

And isn't this where the age-old story began? With no room at the inn?

She, who so desperately wanted to give everyone the perfect Christmas, turning away a stranger on the flimsy excuse that her need for predictability felt threatened by his cynical look and the dark mystery that clung to him like fog clinging to a dark forest?

By the treacherous little niggling of her own attraction? The part of her she would have sworn, even seconds ago, that she had completely tamed?

A primitive longing that if she indulged it, could turn her into her mother in a horrifying blink? Prepared to throw away everything—*every-thing*—for whatever it was that hard mouth promised.

She tried to reason with herself. He needed a place to stay. A few hours. That was hardly going to rock her world, mature business woman that she was now.

She pulled off the Santa hat.

His eyes went to her hair, something twitched along the firm line of his mouth, but then was gone.

"The highway patrol said you have the only ac-commodations in the entire Willowbrook area." The way he said it made her feel as if he would have stayed elsewhere if he'd had a choice.

A modern hotel, stylish and without charac-ter. In his eyes, she saw all her hard work judged harshly, dismissed as corny, not charming. She did not like it one bit that the judgments of a complete stranger could hurt so badly. For a moment she wanted desperately to tell him she did not let rooms in the winter, which she didn't.

But he had no choice. And neither did she. She was not sending that baby back out into the storm.

Despite the fact that none of the normal precautions were in place that protected her as a single woman running a business—the previsit information sheet, the credit card verification of ID—Emma felt only the danger of her attraction.

Something about the way he held the baby, protective, fierce, made her understand the only dangers he posed to her were emotional ones. But even if she were foolish enough to let forced proximity threaten her vows of independence, one look at his shuttered face assured her he would never be foolish.

She stepped back from the door, coolly professional. "I usually don't operate as an inn in the winter, but I can clearly see that this is an emergency."

If she hoped her aloof graciousness would give her the upper hand, she was mistaken. Scent swept in the door with him, the deeply masculine smells of soap and aftershave, the baby scents of powder and purity, quickly overpowering all the warm cookie and Christmas smells.

When she firmly closed the door against the weather, the ancient knob came off in her hand, making her feel not professional, and not gracious, either.

Not now, she warned the old house, stuffing the knob back in the hole, hoping he hadn't noticed.

But when she turned back to him, she could see he was a man who noticed everything. He would have noticed even if the knob had not popped back out of the door and landed with a clatter on the floor.

She bent and picked it up, thoroughly flustered. "I don't charge extra for the rustic charm," she said breezily, trying to ignore the cold air whooshing through the round hole in the door where the knob should have been.

No smile.

"Ah." He glanced around her front foyer, took in the small welcoming hallway tree, decorated entirely in tiny white angels, the garlands of white-bowed boughs that wove their way up the staircase and had, until seconds ago, filled her house with the sharp, fresh scents of pine and Christmas.

He stood directly under the sprig of mistletoe she had suspended from the ceiling, and that made her look at his lips.

And think a distressing thought, entirely inappropriate for an independent professional such as herself, about what they would taste like, and what price a woman would be willing to pay to know that.

Too much. The price would be too much. She was still reeling from her mistake in judgment about Peter. Guessing what a complete stranger's lips might taste like was just proof, as if she needed more, that she was still capable of grave errors.

He frowned. "If you don't operate as an inn at this time of year, do you do all of this decorating for your personal enjoyment?"

"I was expecting guests for the evening." She fought further evidence of her poor judgment—a ridiculous temptation to drop the professional facade and to unburden herself about the disastrous inaugural evening of Holiday Happenings. Though his shoulders looked broad enough to cry on, his eyes did not look capable of sympathy.

His next words made her glad she had kept her confidences. "Do you have any rooms without the, er, Christmas theme?"

"You don't like Christmas." She said it flatly, a statement rather than a question. Given his expression, it was already more than obvious to her he did not like Christmas. And probably not puppies, love songs or tender movies, either.

Which was good. Very good. So much easier to get through a few hours of temptation—of her own bad decision-making abilities—if the effect of those intoxicating good looks were offset by a vile nature.

What kind of person doesn't like Christmas? Especially with a baby! He practically has an obligation to like Christmas!

The baby gurgled, reached up from under the blanket and inserted a pudgy finger in her mouth.

Nothing in the man's expression softened, but the baby didn't seem to notice.

"Mama," the baby whispered, and laid her head on his shoulder in a way that confirmed what Emma already knew. Her guest might be cynical and Christmas-hating, but she could trust him with her life, just as that baby, now slurping contentedly on her thumb, did.

"Is she wanting her mama?" Emma asked,

struck by the backward bonnet again, by the incongruity of this man, seemingly without any kind of softness, being with this baby. *Of course. A mother.* That made her safe from this feeling, hot and liquid, unfurling like a sail catching a wind. He was taken. Her relief, her profound sense of *escape* was short-lived.

"No," he said, and then astonishingly, a flush of red moved up his neck, and Emma saw the tiniest hint of vulnerability in those closed features.

He hesitated, "Unfortunately, that's what she calls me."

Again, Emma felt a tickle of laughter. And again it was cut off before it materialized, because of the unwanted *softness* for him when she thought of him being called Mama. It was a startling contradiction to the forbidding presence of him, ridiculously sweet.

Even though she knew it was none of her business, she *had* to know.

"Where is her mother?"

Something shot through his eyes with such intensity it sucked all the warmth from the room. It was more than sadness, for a moment she glimpsed a soul stripped of joy, of hope. She glimpsed a man lost in a storm far worse than the one that howled outside her door.

"She's dead," he said quietly, and the window that had opened briefly to a tormented soul slammed shut. His voice was flat and calm, his eyes warned her against probing his soul any deeper.

"I'm so sorry," Emma said. "Here, let me take her while you get your coat off."

But when she held out her arms, she realized she was still holding the broken door knob.

He juggled the baby, and took the doorknob with his free hand, his gloved fingers brushing hers just long enough for her to feel the heat beneath those gloves.

Effortlessly, he turned and inserted the knob in the door, jiggled it into place and then turned back to her.

His easy competence made Emma feel more off center, incompetent, as if her stupid doorknob was sending out messages about her every failing as an innkeeper.

"The coat rack is behind you," she said, and then added formally, as if she was the doorman. "Is there luggage?"

"I hope we won't be staying long enough to need it." He handed the baby to her.

Me, too, Emma thought. The baby was surprisingly heavy, her weight sweet and pliable as if she was made of warm pudding, boneless.

The wind picked that moment to howl and rattle the windows, and it occurred to Emma she might be fighting temptation for more than a few hours. It was quite possible her visitors would be here at least the night. Thankfully she thought of the crib she had found so that the babies who came Christmas Day would have a place to nap.

The baby regarded her warily, scrunching up her face in case terror won out over curiosity.

"How old is she?"

"Fourteen months."

"What's her name?" Emma asked softly, grateful for the baby's distraction against the man removing his jacket to reveal a dark, expensive shirt perfectly tailored to fit over those impossibly broad shoulders, dark trousers that accentuated legs that were long, hard-muscled beneath the fine fabric.

"Tess," he provided.

"Hello, Tess," she crooned. "Welcome to the White Christmas Inn. I'm Emma."

"The White Christmas Inn?" the man said, "you aren't serious, are you?"

"Didn't you see the sign on the driveway?" Just this morning, she had placed the word *Christmas* over the word *Pond,* the letters of *Christmas* just the teensiest bit squished to make them fit.

"I saw a sign, I assumed it was for the inn, but most of it is covered in snow and ice."

"The White Christmas Inn. Seriously."

He groaned, softly.

"Is there a problem?"

His answer was rhetorical. "Do you ever feel the gods like to have a laugh at the plans of human beings?"

Even though he obviously expected no answer, Emma responded sadly, "Yes. Yes, I do."

The White Christmas Inn.

Ryder Richardson had no doubt the gods *were* enjoying a robust laugh at his expense right now. When he had headed out on the road tonight, he'd had one goal: to escape Christmas entirely.

He had packed up his niece, Tess, and that amazing mountain of things that accompanied a traveling baby, with every intention of making it to his lakeside cottage by dark.

The cottage where there would be absolutely no ho-ho-ho, no colorful lights, no carols, no tree, no people and especially no phone. He had deliberately left his cell phone at home. Ryder Richardson could make Scrooge look like a bit player in the bah-humbug department.

He was not ashamed to admit to himself he just wanted to hide out until it was all over. Until the trees were shredded into landscape pulp, the lights were down, there was not a carol to be heard, and he could walk along a sidewalk without hearing bells or having complete strangers smile at him and wish him a Merry Christmas.

Ryder looked forward to the dreary days of January like a man on a ship watching for a beacon to keep him from the rocks on the darkest night.

In January there would be fewer reminders and fewer calls offering sympathy. The invitations to holiday parties and dinners and events designed to lure him out of his memories and his misery would die down.

In his luggage, he had made a small concession to Christmas. Ryder had a few simple gifts to give Tess. He had a soft stuffed pony in an implausible shade of lavender, new pink suede shoes, for she already shared a woman's absolute delight in footwear, and a small, hardy piano-like toy that he was probably going to regret obtaining within hours of having given it to her.

He had not brought wrapping paper, and probably would not give Tess the gifts on December twenty-fifth, taking advantage of the fact that at fourteen months of age his niece was not aware enough of the concept of Christmas to know the difference.

This would be his year of reprieve. Next year, Tess would be two at Christmas. It wouldn't be so easy to pretend the season didn't exist. Next year, she would probably have grasped the whole concept of Santa, would *want* things from Ryder. Would he be able to give them to her?

As he turned back from the coat rack, through the open archway from the foyer into the living room, he caught sight of the fire burning brightly in the hearth at the White Christmas Inn, the huge tree glowing, top to bottom, an ethereal shade of white.

Despite steeling himself against all things Christmas, the scene called to him, like the lights of home calling a warrior back to his own land. For a disturbing moment he felt almost pulled toward that room, the tree, the promise it held. *Hope.*

CHAPTER TWO

HOPE. The word burned in Ryder's heart for a second or two, not bright and warm, but painful. Because that was what he was intent on quashing in himself. He was a warrior who had glimpsed the lights of a home he could never go back to.

The socks that hung from the mantel, cheerful, were what triggered the memory.

Without warning—for the memories always came without warning, riding in on a visual clue or a scent or a sound he could not control—a picture flashed in his mind of different socks on a different mantel nearly a year ago. Those socks, bright red, with white fur cuffs, had names on them.

Drew. Tracy. Tess.

Ryder could see his brother, standing in front

of those socks, holding the tiny baby way above his head, bringing her down, her round belly to his lips, blowing, the baby gurgling, and Drew looking as happy as Ryder had ever seen his brother look.

A shudder rippled through Ryder, and he looked deliberately away from the socks that hung on the mantel of the White Christmas Inn, picked up the baby bag that he had dropped on the floor, shrugged it over his shoulder.

In a few days, a year would have passed, and Ryder's pain had not been reduced. A reminder about the danger of hope. There was no sense hoping next year would be better. There was no sense hoping life could ever be what it had been before the fire that had swept through his brother's house early Christmas morning.

"Get the baby," Drew had cried to him, as he'd stumbled out of the guest room, "I'll get Tracy."

Anyone who had not been in a fire could not understand the absolute and disorienting darkness, the heat, the smoke, the chaos intensified by the roar and shriek of it, as if the fire was a living thing, a monster, a crazed animal.

Somehow, Ryder had found the baby, and

gotten her outside. Tracy had already been out there, in bad shape, burned, dazed, barely coherent. At first Ryder thought that meant his brother was safe. But then he'd realized Drew was still in there, looking for his wife, not knowing she was out here.

He'd raced back for the door, uncaring that flames roared out of it like it was the mouth of hell. He'd almost made it, too, back in there to find his brother.

But neighbors had pulled him back, four men, and then six, holding him, dodging his fists, absorbing his punches, their urgency to keep him out of there as great as his to go back in. He still woke in the night sometimes, coated in sweat, his heart beating hard, screaming his fury.

Let me go. You don't understand. Let...me... go.

When Ryder thought of that the fury was fresh. If anything, he added to it as time went on. How could he have failed so terribly? How could his strength have failed him when he needed it most? If he could have shaken off those men, made them understand...

Then, just three months ago, more heartbreak,

an intensified sense of failure, as Tracy, all out of bravery, had quit fighting her horrible injuries.

If there was a feeling Ryder hated more than any other it was that one: *powerlessness*. He'd been as powerless to save Tracy as he had been to break free of the men who had kept him from his brother.

Ryder shuddered again. He had put a wall around himself, and instead of letting it come down as time passed, brick by brick he made it stronger. He was ravaged by what had happened, destroyed by it. He could function, but not feel.

He hated it that his armor felt threatened by the fact that, ever so briefly, he had *felt* what the room had to offer. Heard the word. *Hope.* And seen that other word on her front door.

Believe.

"Are you all right?"

"Yes," he said, keeping his voice deliberately cold, protecting the coating of ice that shielded what was left of his heart.

No, he wasn't. He had tried to keep Christmas, its association with his greatest failure, at bay. Instead, at the caprice of fate, here he was at a place that appeared to have more Christmas than the North Pole. If there were no baby to think of, he would put his coat back on and take his chances with the storm.

But then, if there were no baby to think of, he was pretty sure he would have self-destructed already.

"You looked like you saw a ghost," Emma said. "Apparently we have them here, but I haven't seen one yet."

She actually sounded envious that he might have spotted one.

"I don't believe in ghosts," he said curtly. Did she notice the emphasis on *believe?* Because that was the first in a long list of things he did not believe in. He hoped he would not be here long enough to share the full extent of his disillusionment with her.

"Well, I do," she said, a hint of something stubborn in her voice. "I think there are spirits around this old house that protect it and the people in it. And I think there is a spirit of Christmas, too."

And then, having made her stand, she blushed.

He looked at her carefully. Now that she had taken the hat off, he felt much less inclined to ask to speak to her mother. How old would she be? Early twenties, probably. Too young to be running this place, and too old to be believing nonsense.

He replayed her words of earlier. *I usually don't operate as an inn in the winter. I don't charge extra for the rustic charm.*

I not *we.*

She ran a hand through the dark, wild hair revealed by the removal of the awful Santa hat, a gesture that was self-conscious. Her blush was deepening.

Despite the shard of the memory stuck in his heart like broken glass, her hair tried, for the second time, to take down a brick, to tease something out of him. A smile? Only Tess made him smile. Though her hair was worse than Tess's, which was saying something. His hostess's hair, dark and shiny, was a tangle of dark coils, flattened by the hat, but looking as if they intended to spring back up at any moment.

He was shocked by the slipping of another brick—an impulse to touch her hair, to coax the curls up with his fingertips. He killed the impulse before it even fully formed, but not before he pictured how encouraging the wild disarray of her hair would make her sexy, rather than the adorable image the red socks and red sweater projected.

She was looking at him like a kitten ready to show claws if he chose to argue the spirit of Christmas with her, which he didn't.

If the way she held Tess and crooned to her was any indication, she was exactly as she appeared; soft, wholesome, slightly eccentric, a *believer* in goodness and light and spirits protecting her house and Christmas. Not his type at all.

Even back in the day, before *it* had happened, when he cared about such things, he'd gone for flashier women, whitened teeth, diamond rings, designer clothes. Women who would have scorned this place as hokey, and his hostess for being so naive.

Except, last year, a spectator to the domestic bliss his brother had found, Ryder had thought, briefly, *maybe I want this, too.*

But now he knew he didn't want anything that intensified that feeling of being powerless, and in his mind that's what being open to another person would do, make him weak instead of strong, slowly but surely erode the bricks of his defenses. What was behind that wall was grief and fury so strong he had no doubt it would destroy him and whoever was close to him, if and when it ever came out.

For Tess's sake, as well as his own, he kept a lid on *feelings*. He knew he had nothing to give anyone; somehow he was hoping his niece would be the exception, though he had no idea how she would be.

"You don't run this place by yourself, do you?" he asked, suddenly needing to know, not liking the idea of being alone with all this sweetness, not trusting himself with it, especially after that renegade impulse to tease something sexy out of her hair.

He hoped, suddenly, for a family-run operation, for parents in the wings, or better yet, a husband. Someone to kill dead this enemy within him, the unexpected sizzle of attraction he felt. Someone he could talk hockey with as the night dragged on, to keep his mind off how little he wanted to be here, and how little fate cared about what he wanted.

Ryder's eyes drifted to her ring finger. Red nail polish, a bit of a surprise, but probably chosen in the spirit of the season, to match the socks. How could he possibly be finding this woman, who stood for everything he was trying to run away from, attractive?

There was no ring on her finger, so he knew the answer to his question even before she answered.

"It's all mine," she said, and her chin lifted proudly. "I inherited the house from my grandmother, restored it, named it the White Pond Inn, and have been operating it on my own ever since."

"I thought it was the White Christmas Inn," he reminded her dryly.

"Christmas transforms everything," she said with grave dignity, "it makes all things magic, even my humble inn."

Well, she obviously *believed.*

"Uh-huh." He didn't want to get into it. He truly didn't want to know a single thing more about her. He didn't want to *like* the fact that despite her corkscrew hair waiting to pop into action, and despite her falling-off doorknob, she was trying so hard to keep her dignity.

Show me to my room. Please. But somehow, instead, Ryder found himself asking, "What makes a young woman tackle a project like this?" He didn't add, *on her own,* though that was really his question.

Ryder was an architect. He and Drew had drawn up plenty of plans to restore places like this one. Underneath all the cosmetic loveliness, he was willing to bet the abundance of decorations hid what the falling-off door handle had hinted at. Problems. Large and small. Way more than a little scrap of a woman on her own would be up to.

"I'm a dreamer," she said, fiercely unapologetic, and again, in the way she said that, he caught sight of her pride and stubbornness. And her hurt. As if someone—probably a hard-hearted jerk like him—had mocked her for being a dreamer.

Whoo boy. He bit his tongue, because it was obvious to him this house did not need a dreamer. A carpenter, certainly. Likely an electrician. Probably a plumber.

Despite biting his tongue nearly clear through, his skepticism must have clearly shown on his face because she felt driven to convince him—or maybe herself—that the house *needed* a dreamer.

"I actually saw it for the first time when my grandmother got sick. My mother and she had been, um, estranged, but one of the neighbors called and asked me to come home to help care for her. This house was love at first sight for me. Plus, it had been in our family for generations. When Granny died, I inherited, and I had to figure out a way I could afford to keep it."

That was a warning, if he'd ever heard one. He did not like women who believed in love at first sight. As a man who lived in the wreckage of dreams, he did not like dreamers nor all their infuriating optimism.

Aside from that, the words told him an even more complete truth, whether he wanted to know it or not, and he didn't. He saw the glitter of some defense in her eyes that told him things he would have been just as happy not knowing.

Hurt. Clues in what she was telling him. Something missing in her family, that had filled her with longing? Despite the happy Christmas costume, there was a reason a woman like that took on a place like this. And he was willing to bet it had little to do with family heritage, and a whole lot to (broken heart. She had decided loving a house was easier than loving a person.

He heartily approved, though he wondered if a dreamer could be pragmatic enough to pull that off.

This ability to *see* people more clearly than they wanted to be seen, and certainly more clearly than he wanted to see them, was one of the things Ryder hated since the fire. He sensed things, often seeing *past* what people said, to some truth about them. It was a cruel irony, since he was desperately trying not to care about anything, that he could see things he had never seen before, things that threatened the walls and armor of the defenses that kept some things in him, and some things out.

Pre-fire, Ryder had been a typical man, happily superficial, involved totally in himself. Building a business with his brother, hanging out with his buddies, playing in a semi-serious hockey league, and never getting even semi-serious with any one woman. That had been his life: a happy, carefree place. A guy zone of self-centered hedonism.

He had never been deep. *Insensitive* probably

would have described him nicely, blissfully unaware there was any other way to be.

Now, he could walk by a complete stranger, and see their tragedies in the lines around their mouths and the shadows in their eyes. It was as if he had become a member of a secret club of sadness. *Not* seeing had been a blessing he had not appreciated at the time.

A little more than a year ago, Ryder certainly wouldn't have ever been able to spot the hurt hiding in the shadows of Emma's eyes. He realized, uncomfortably, that even with those shadows, her eyes were amazing.

A part of him, purely masculine, acknowledged that physically Emma was exquisite. Her features were small and perfect, her nose snubbed up a touch at the end, her lips formed plump bows of sensuality. And he was not sure he had ever quite seen that shade of eye color before, soft gray-green, moss and mist.

Despite the outfit—was it deliberately chosen to hide her assets? Another thing he probably would not have guessed pre-fire—he could see she was delicately curved, unconsciously sensuous.

Annoyed with himself, he realized it was the first time since the fire he had allowed the faint stir of attraction toward a member of the opposite sex to penetrate his barriers.

Strange it would be her. The women he had been attracted to in the past were as superficial as he was. He had liked women who wore clingy clothes, and push-up bras, who glittered with makeup and jewelry, and who intoxicated with expensive scents.

Emma had probably wiggled by his defenses simply because he would have never thought to erect that particular wall against someone like her: makeup-free, tangled hair, lumpy jeans, grandma sweater. And defiantly set on letting him know she *believed*.

Still, regardless of how she had done it, it had happened. That faint stirring of something, that felt like life. Trying to call him back.

To a place, he reminded himself sternly, that was gone.

He shut down what he was feeling, quickly, but he could not shut down the acknowledgment that it had been a first. He did not feel ready for firsts: to laugh again, to feel again.

Because somehow even contemplating the possibility of firsts, of returning, felt like some kind of betrayal, as if it minimized who Drew and Tracy had been and what they had meant to him. And maybe because it would require him to do what could not be done: forgive himself.

So, in a different lifetime, when he had been a different man, Ryder might have followed that thread of attraction to see where it would lead.

But he already knew Emma was hurt, had already seen secrets in her soft eyes that she probably would rather he not have known.

And the man he was now was so damaged that he knew he could only hurt her more. His hardness felt as though it would take all that was wondrous about her—such as this childlike delight in Christmas—and curdle it, like vinegar hitting milk.

It was all the smells in here, pine and pumpkin, all the decorations, her ridiculous hat making her look like an emissary from Santa, that were bringing up these uncomfortable thoughts. For the most part, Ryder was successful at warding off the worst of it.

Still, that all this had flooded in within

moments of entering this place troubled him. He would probably be better off sleeping in his car than taking refuge here.

He'd known as soon as he stepped under the roof of her porch that this place posed a peculiar kind of danger to his armored heart. As if to confirm that suspicion, he had spotted the letters, peeking out from under the boughs of the wreath.

Believe.

The sign had made him want to head back to his car, find shelter elsewhere. *Believe in what?*

If he'd been by himself, he would have gone back to the car, found a pub, preferably with a pool table and a big-screen TV, to while away the hours in before the road reopened.

But he wasn't by himself, and the fact that he wasn't changed his ability to choose.

Every single decision Ryder made had to be run through the filter of what was best for Tess. Obviously it wasn't a place with a pool table, however comforting he would have found a rowdy male environment.

What was best for Tess? In the long run? He knew people wondered if he could possibly be the best guardian for her. Some of the bolder ones had even hinted that the most loving thing to do would be to find her a real family, a mother who could actually get a comb through her hair, who would enjoy the intricacies of those silly, frilly, small dresses.

But his brother and Tracy had wanted him to have her. He'd been stunned that they'd had a will, that they had appointed him guardian.

Despite the fact he knew himself to be terribly flawed, Ryder could not ever let her go. Tess was what was left of his brother. He was fierce in his protection of her. He hired a nanny who looked after the baby details—hair, baths, clothes—but Mrs. Markle had abandoned him for Christmas to be with her own family.

His initial awkwardness with the baby had quickly given way to absolute devotion. What was left of his heart belonged firmly to that little spark of spirit that represented all that was left of Drew and Tracy's great love for each other.

"I can show you to a room, or take you through to the kitchen to get something to eat first."

Tess had nursed a bottle in the car, but could use something solid. But Ryder realized he was also starving. And exhausted from fighting with the roads. If he had something to eat and a nap, he would be ready to leave here the second there was a break in the weather and the roads reopened.

"Something to eat sounds good." He could feel his own caution, as if even agreeing to have something to eat was tampering with forces he was not ready to tamper with.

"It must have been a nightmare out there," his hostess said, still lugging Tess, leading him down a narrow hallway that ended in a swinging door. She gave it a push with her hip.

"A nightmare," he agreed. "Hell, only the cold version, decorated in white." *Something like her inn.*

She didn't miss the reference to white decorations, and he saw her take his comment like a blow, as a personal insult. Too sensitive. Was that why she'd been hurt?

"Nothing against white decorations," he said curtly, his insincerity just making everything worse.

Vinegar and milk, he told himself.

He wanted to say he wasn't hungry, after all. Wanted to retreat to a room, hoping it wouldn't be too overwhelmingly Chrismasified, but the truth was, now that he was not battling his way through terrible conditions, he was ravenous.

And even if he wasn't, the baby had to eat something out of one of those little jars of mash he carried with him.

His initial relief that the kitchen was an oasis of "not decorated" evaporated. The smells were intense in this room, as was the atmosphere of country cheer and charm: sunshine-yellow walls, white cabinets, old gray linoleum floors polished to high gloss. But, like the door handle falling off, he could see hints of problems, frost on the inside of the windows, a tap dripping.

A huge plank harvest table dominated the room and was covered in platters and platters of cookies.

On a closer look, there were cookies shaped like trees, and cookies frosted in pink, Santa cookies, and chocolate-dipped cookies, ginger-bread men and gingerbread houses.

"You weren't kidding that you were expecting guests," he said. "How many?"

"I was hoping for a hundred."

He shot her a wary look at the disappointment

in her voice. "You were expecting a hundred people here tonight?"

"The opening night of Holiday Happenings," she said, and he did his best to remain expressionless at how horrifying he found that name. She took his silence, unfortunately, as an invitation to go on, even though her voice had begun to wobble.

"There's a pond out back. There was going to be skating. And bonfires. A neighbor was going to bring his team of horses. Clydesdales." Something was shining behind her eyes.

He thought, again, of the kind of women he had once dated. Five-star meals, gifts of diamonds, evenings that ended in hot tubs. Not Holiday Happenings kind of women.

Emma's disappointment was palpable. He hoped, uneasily and fervently, she wasn't going to cry. Nothing felt like a threat to him as much as a woman's tears. Tess already knew, and used it to her advantage at every opportunity.

"Sorry," he said, gruffly, whether he meant it or because he hoped saying something—anything— could curb her distress, he wasn't sure.

"Things will be back to normal by tomorrow," she said, "Holiday Happenings is going to happen."

This was said fiercely as if she was challenging him—or the gods—to disagree with her. He wasn't going to, but the gods seemed to enjoy a challenge like that one.

It was Tess who took Emma's mind off her weather woes. Apparently the baby was tired of looking at the embarrassment of riches around her, and tired of the adult chatter.

She began squealing and pointing at various cookies and nearly wiggled herself right out of Emma's arms.

"WA DAT."

"Want that?" Emma guessed, mercifully distracted. "She's hungry."

"Or could squeeze in a cookie after demolishing a ten-course meal," he said, thanking Tess for evaporating the tears that had shone so briefly behind those eyes.

"Can she have one, daddy? Or does she have to have healthy stuff first?"

He frowned. Let it go? He wasn't going to be here long enough for it to matter, was he? Correcting her meant revealing something more of the private life, fresh with tragedy, that he kept so guarded.

On the other hand, revealing the fact he was not Tess's father seemed safer than returning to the possibility the weather could ruin her plans for Holiday Happenings.

If he never heard the words *Holiday Happenings* again, he would be just as happy. It was worth it, even if it revealed a little of himself.

He realized he had not introduced himself.

"I'm Ryder Richardson," he said, not trying to disguise his reluctance, "I'm Tess's uncle. Her guardian."

"Oh."

It asked questions, none of which he intended to answer. He stuck out his hand, a diversionary tactic to stall questions and to keep her mind off her failed evening.

She juggled the baby, and took his hand. As soon as he felt her hand in his, he knew he'd made a mistake. Her hand slipped inside his, a perfect fit, softness intermingled with surprising strength.

He felt the *zing* of the physical contact, steeled himself against it.

She felt something, too, because she froze for a moment, stared up into his eyes, blinked with startled awareness. And then she pulled her hand away, rapidly.

His eyes went to her lips. Once upon a time, a long time ago, when he was a different man in a different life, he had known other diversionary tactics. Most of them involved lips. His and hers.

Now as profoundly committed to taking his wandering mind off lips as he was to taking Emma's mind off personal questions and the weather, he held out his arms, and Emma gave Tess back to him.

Babies were the grand diversion when it came to women. One look at Tess's hair should take Emma's mind irrevocably off her crushed hopes for the evening, and maybe off that sizzling moment of awareness that had just passed between them.

He propped Tess on the edge of the plank table, removed the blanket, pulled Tess's little limbs from the car coat he'd had her in. Last he fumbled with the ridiculously hard-to-reach snap on the stupid snow hat that he had put on the baby out of a sense of wanting to do the responsible thing before they left on their road trip.

That was the worry part. A snow hat inside the car. In case. Well, that, and to cover the mess of her hair in case they stopped anywhere along the way. The cop might have even looked at him differently if he had spotted the baby's hair.

If you can't even look after her hair, how can you be trusted with the larger picture?

"I hate this hat," he muttered, though what he really hated was that question.

"Why's that?"

"It never seems to go on right."

"Ah." It was a strangled sound.

Ryder shot her a look. She was smiling, biting back a giggle.

He glared at her. He disliked merriment nearly as much as Christmas, especially when it was at his expense and made him feel self-conscious about his baby skills. "Is something funny?" he asked, annoyed.

She held up a finger, letting him know that soon she would be in control of herself. Really, she looked like an evil elf, gasping. The more she tried to stop laughing, the more she couldn't, as if his disapproval was making her nervous. Which was good.

"You…have…it…on…backwards."

He could look at it in a different way. Not that she was laughing at him, but that he'd succeeded. The sparkle of tears were gone from her eyes, replaced, that quickly, with the sparkle of laughter.

Only he hadn't really succeeded. Because he could clearly see she didn't look like an evil elf, after all. The laughter chased some shadow from her eyes, making them even prettier, and the smile made him even more aware of the sensuous lilt of those puffy lips.

He'd been here less than ten minutes, long enough to know he hated the White Christmas Inn and everything about it.

Ryder looked away from her, frowning. He stepped back from Tess and studied the hat. "I'll be damned. It *is* on backwards. No wonder it was so hard to work with."

A respected architect and he couldn't get a hat on right. He was learning babies were an exercise in humility. Experimentally, he turned the headgear around the right way, admired it, allowed a small whisper of pleasure at this tiny discovery.

"It was the placement of the pom-pom that threw me," he decided gravely.

"Of course," she said, just as gravely.

"Now I won't have to buy another hat," he said, allowing that little whisper of pleasure to deepen.

He saw Emma's look, and was astounded at how his pride was stung at her misinterpretation. "Not because I can't afford another one," he said sharply, "because you cannot imagine how terrible it is being the sole man shopping in the baby department."

Tess was crankily trying to pull that hat back off.

"It doesn't look like she likes hats, anyway," Emma said.

"Until she lets me comb her hair, she wears hats." He took the hat back off and stepped aside, letting Emma see for the first time what was underneath.

If she started laughing at him again, he was going to pick up the baby and head back into the storm, knock on the door of the first house in Willowbrook that had no Christmas decorations and beg for sanctuary from the storm.

But Emma didn't laugh. Her gasp of dismay was almost worse.

Hey, it's not as if your hair is all that different.

But Emma's hair *was* different from Tess's. Emma's curls looked as if she had *tried,* maybe too vigorously, to tame them. He felt that inexplicable urge to touch again, focused on his niece's hair instead.

Tess's white blonde hair did not look as if it had been combed since the day she was born, even though it had only been two days. Her hair looked like it belonged to a monster baby.

It formed fuzzy dreadlocks and tortured corkscrews. There was a clump at the back that looked like it might house mice, and two distinct hair horns stood up on either side of her head.

"No nanny for the last two days," he explained, feeling the deep sting of his own ineptitude. "And in Tess's world, Uncle is not allowed to touch the goldilocks."

Emma looked skeptical, as if he might be making up a story to explain away his own negligence.

"I know," he said dryly. "It's shameful. A

twenty pound scrap of baby controlling a full grown man, but there you have it."

Emma still looked skeptical, so he demonstrated. He reached out with one finger. He touched Tess's hair, feather-light, barely a touch at all.

The baby inhaled a deep breath, and exhaled a blood-curdling shriek, as if he dropped a red-hot coal down her diaper. He removed his finger, the shriek stopped abruptly, like a sentence stopped in the middle. Tess regarded him with her most innocent look.

"Ha," he said, moved his finger toward her, and away, shriek, stop, shriek, stop. Soon, he stopped as soon as her mouth opened wide, so she was making O's and closing them, like a fish.

Emma snorted with laughter. Not that he wanted to get her laughing again or explore the intrigue of shadows that danced away when she laughed, and flitted back when she didn't.

Again, he wondered what he was doing. He had not wanted Emma to cry. He wanted this even less. *Firsts.*

There was something tempting about being with someone who did not know his history, as if he could pretend to be a brand-new man. He contemplated that, being free, even for a moment a man unburdened, a man with no history.

But he wasn't those things and Ryder hated himself for thinking he should be free of the mantle he carried. His brother had died because he was, quite simply, not enough.

The fact that Emma could tempt him to feel otherwise made him angry at her as well as at himself, as irrational as that might have been.

CHAPTER THREE

INSTEAD of moving toward the temptation, the *pretense*, of being a man he was not, Ryder mentally reshouldered his burdens, and stopped playing the little game with Tess, but not before he felt that small sigh of gratitude that his niece did bring some lightness into a world gone dark.

"Can she have a cookie?" Emma asked, coming back to her original question.

"I'll try her with a little baby food first." He dug through the bag, and a bottle dropped to the floor. He watched it roll downhill, another indicator the house was hiding some major problems.

Which were, he noted thankfully, none of his concern. He fetched the bottle back, and got out a jar, which he heated in the microwave for a few seconds.

But, of course, the baby food proved impossible, Tess wiggling around in the high chair Emma had unearthed and focused totally on the cookies that surrounded her. She swatted impatiently when he tried to deliver pureed carrots to her.

"Certified organic, too," he said, finally quitting, wiping a splotch of carrot off his shirt. "She had a bottle in the car a while ago, so go ahead, give her a cookie."

Unmindful that the baby was now covered in carrots, including some in the tangle of hair he was not allowed to touch, Emma swooped her up from the high chair.

"Which one, Tess?" Emma asked, stopping at each plate, letting his niece inspect.

Tess chose a huge gingerbread man, picked a jelly bean off his belly and gobbled it up.

"You must be hungry, too," Emma said to him. "I can't offer anything fancy. I have hot dogs for Holiday Happenings."

No! After all his work at distraction, they were right back to this? The shadow in her eyes darkened every time she mentioned her weather-waylaid event.

"If you'd like a glass of mulled wine or hot

chocolate, I have several gallons of both at the warming shed."

Several gallons of wine sounded terribly attractive.

An escape he did not allow himself. Tess needed better.

"A couple of hot dogs would be perfect." He watched Tess polish off the jelly-bean buttons and take a mighty bite of her gingerbread man's head. Disappointment registered on her face as she chewed.

"YUCK." Without ceremony she spat out what was in her mouth, tossed the headless gingerbread man on the floor and reached for a different cookie.

Emma thought it was funny, but these were the challenges in his life. What was best for Tess? Was she too young to try and teach her manners? Did he just accept the fact she didn't like the cookie and let it go? Or by doing nothing was he teaching her the lifelong habit of smashing cookies on the floor?

Serial smasher.

Ryder rubbed at his forehead. He could convince himself he did okay on the big things for Tess: providing a home, clothing, food, a lovely middle-aged nanny who loved his niece to distraction. But it was always the little things, cookies and bonnets, that made him wonder what the hell he was doing.

People had the audacity to hint he needed a partner, a wife, a feminine influence for Tess, but to him the fact they suggested it only meant he had become successful at hiding how broken he was inside. What little he had left to give he was saving for Tess, and he hoped it would be enough.

Suddenly he felt too tired and too hungry even to think.

Or to defend himself against the thought that came.

That he was alone in the world. That all the burdens of the past and all the decisions about the future were his alone to carry and to make.

The warmth of the White Christmas Inn was creeping inside him, despite his efforts to keep it at bay, making him feel *more* alone.

Emma had said Christmas transformed everything and made it magic, and she had said there were spirits here who protected all who entered. But the last thing he needed was to be so tired and hungry that her whimsy could seep past the formidable wall of his defenses.

So what if he didn't have what most people were able to take for granted? So what if life was unfair? He already knew that better than most. So, he didn't have someone to ask about the baby spitting out a cookie, he didn't have a holiday season to look forward to instead of dread, he didn't have a place to belong that was somehow more than walls and furniture. He had made his choice. Not to rely on anyone or anything, because he of all people knew that those things could be taken in an instant.

Loss had left him weakened, more loss would finish him. He had a responsibility. He was all Tess had left in the world. He wasn't leaving himself open to the very forces that had nearly destroyed him already.

Ryder Richardson needed desperately to be strong for the little girl who had fallen asleep in Emma's arms, one mashed half-eaten cookie still clutched in a grubby fist.

He felt his strength returning after he ate the hot dogs and about two dozen of the cookies. But inside he felt crabby about this situation he found himself in. He had made himself a world without tests, and he felt as if he was being tested.

Make that *crabbier.*

"Thanks for the meal," he said, formally. "If you could show me our room, Tess needs to be put in a bed, and I need to check the weather."

"I don't quite know how to break this to you," whatever she was about to break to him delighted her, he noticed with annoyance, "but the only way you'll be checking the weather from your room is by sticking your head out the window."

For a moment he didn't quite grasp what she was saying. And when he did, the sensation of crabbiness, of his life being wrested out of his control, intensified.

No television in the room. No escape, no way of turning off everything going on inside him. He considered the television the greatest tool ever invented for numbing wayward feelings, for acting as anesthetic for a doubting mind.

"People come here to get away from it all," she said cheerfully.

"To feel the magic," he said, faintly sarcastic.

"Precisely," she said happily, he suspected missing his sarcasm deliberately.

"You have a television somewhere, right?"

"Well, yes, but—"

"No buts. Lead me to it. Or face the wrath of man."

She didn't seem to find his pun funny at all. And he was glad. He really didn't need to experience Emma's laughter again. Especially if he was going to stay strong.

The wrath of man. Funny. Except he meant it. And there was something in him, something fierce and closed, that reminded Emma of a warrior. There was no doubt in her mind he would lay down his life for the baby that so obviously held his hardened heart in the pudgy pink palm of her hand.

The baby had clearly—and gleefully—demonstrated her power with the hilarious hair show.

But whatever moment of lightness he had allowed himself then was gone from Ryder's face now. He was practically bristling with bad temper.

It would be a foolish time to let him know that

television was not part of Emma's vision for the White Pond Inn, and it certainly didn't fit in with its incarnation as the White Christmas Inn.

But she had already told him she believed in spirits and magic, risking Ryder's scorn because she had vowed, after Peter, there would be no more trying to hide who she *really* was from other people, no more giving opinions that they wanted to hear.

What an expert she had become at reading what Peter wanted from the faintest purse of lips, giving that to him, making him happy at her own expense. How many times had she swallowed back what she really wanted to say so as not to risk his disapproval, his patronizing suggestions for her "improvement"?

"I consider the inn a techno-electro-free zone," she said, and could hear a certain fierceness in her own voice, as if somehow it was this man's fault that even after she had nearly turned herself inside-out trying to please Peter, he had still searched for someone more suitable. And found her.

"Techno-electro," he said, mulling over the word, which she was pretty sure she had just invented.

"Television is not on the activities agenda, not even on the bad-weather days."

"I'm dying to know what you do on the bad-weather days."

Even though he clearly wasn't, she forged on, determined to be herself. "I bring out board games, and a selection of jigsaw puzzles. I always have tons of books around. I encourage guests to shut off their cell phones and leave the laptops at home."

She crossed her arms over her chest, daring him to find her corny while almost hoping he would. Because if he judged her the way Peter had judged her she could dismiss the somewhat debilitating attraction she felt for him.

She realized she was a little disappointed when he didn't even address her philosophy.

"Since I'm here by the force of fate, instead of by choice, you're going to make an exception for me."

It wasn't a question, and he was absolutely right. He had not come here looking for what her other guests came here looking for. He was not enchanted, and he had no intention of being brought under the spell of the White Christmas Inn.

Which was good. What would she do with a man like that under her spell?

"I do have a television in my room," she admitted reluctantly.

What she didn't admit to was the DVD player. They were guilty pleasures she indulged in when she was just too exhausted to do even one more thing. There was always something to be done when you ran an establishment like this: windows to be cleaned, bedding to be laundered, floors to be polished, flower beds, lawns, paint-touchups. And that was just the day-to-day chores and didn't include the catastrophes, like the time the upstairs bathtub had fallen through the floor.

Sometimes, it was true, on those bad-weather days while her guests played games, she watched a growing collection of romantic movies. She saw them as a replacement for emotional entanglement, not a longing for it.

"Your room? That's the only television in the house?" The thought of entering her bedroom clearly made him as uncomfortable as it made her.

The very thought of those dark warrior eyes taking in the details of her room made her heart beat a fast and traitorous tempo. Her room matched the theme of Christmas: white, though that was how her room was year-round. The walls were the color of rich dairy cream, there was a thick white duvet on the gorgeous bed, an abundance of white pillows in delicious rich textures and fabrics.

When she walked in, the room always seemed soft to her, as comforting as a feather pillow.

But when she saw it through his eyes, she wondered what he would see. And the thought came to her: virginal.

A warrior and a virgin.

She nearly choked on the renegade thought, told herself she had been reading a few too many of the romance novels, more replacements, so much safer and more predictable than real-life romance. She kept a nice selection in tidy stacks on her bedside table, right beside the much-watched DVDs.

But it would make her feel altogether too vulnerable for him to see that, since he might misinterpret her fascination with a certain style of book and film as longing rather than what it was.

"I'll go get the television for you. You'd be more comfortable watching it down here than in my room." And then she blushed as if discussing her room was akin to discussing her panties. Which might be lying on the floor, one of the relaxed slips of the single life.

"I can carry it for you."

"No, no," she protested, too strenuously, "it's tiny."

"That figures," he said, still grouchy, having no problem at all being himself. Which was grouchy and cynical and Christmas-hating. It really balanced out the formidable attraction of his good looks quite remarkably.

"Make yourself comfortable." She handed the sleeping baby back to him, dislodging the cookie from the fist first. "Go into the great room. Through there. I'll be down in a sec."

She hoped her room would have the calming effect on her that it always did. But it didn't. There were no panties on the floor, of course, because she liked the room to look perfect, but even still, instead of being her soothing sanctuary, her sea of textured white softness seemed sensual, like a bridal chamber.

She realized she had been reading too many books, watching too many glorious movies, because totally unbidden her mind provided her with a picture of what he might look like here, lying on that bed, naked from the waist up, holding his arms out to her, his eyes holding smoldering welcome. She shivered at the heat of the picture, at the animal stab of desire she felt.

Your mother was a wild child, Tim had told her sadly, when she had been crushed by Lynelle's absence at her own mother's funeral. *It was like an illness she was born with. Nothing around these parts ever interested her or was good enough for her.*

Peter's mother had not warmed to Emma when they had finally met on that disastrous Christmas Day last year. Emma had felt acutely that when Mrs. Henderson looked at her, she disapproved of something. Make that everything.

"Stop it," Emma ordered herself sternly. Just because you had a wild child in you didn't mean you had to be owned by it, the way her mother had been. It was not part of being herself. In fact, it was something she intended to fight.

So she swept the romance novels off the bedside table and shoved them under the bed. Then, realizing it could just as easily be another symptom of make-yourself-over-so-other-people-will-like-you, as of fighting-the-wild-child, she fished them back out and stood holding them, not sure what to do.

This is what a man did! Disrupted a perfectly contented life. She set the books on the table and planted the DVDs right on top of them.

Ryder Richardson was not coming into this room. Why was she acting as if he would ever see this? He was a stranger, and despite the harsh judgments in Mrs. Henderson's eyes, and despite her mother's example, Emma was not the kind of woman who conducted dalliances with strangers, no matter how attractive they were. No matter how attractive their helpless devotion for a baby.

Still, despite the fact Emma was definitely not conducting a dalliance, she quickly divested herself of the long johns under her jeans. They were not making her feel just bulky, but also hot and bothered.

Wait, maybe that was him!

Despite the fact she'd ordered herself not to, she spent a moment more trying to do something with hair made crazier by the Santa hat.

"Tess and I would tie for first place in the bad-hair-day contest," she told herself, combing some curl conditioner through her hair. The flattened curls sprang up as though she had stuck her finger in a socket, not exactly the effect she'd been looking for.

On the other hand, she was not conducting a dalliance, so the worse she looked the better, right? She was hardly a temptation!

And never had been. When Peter's old girlfriend, Monique, had reentered the picture, he had gone back to her.

And blamed Emma! Her attention to the inn had caused him to be unfaithful. It hadn't been his fault, it had been *hers*.

She left the room, that memory fresh enough that no member of the male species was going to look attractive to her! Then she had to go back for the television she had gone up for in the first place.

Trying to look only composed, *indifferent*, neither a wild child nor a woman scorned, she moved into the great room, placed the TV on a small rosewood end table and plugged it in.

She needn't have worried about her hair. Or about being seduced by a warrior. Or about giving in to her own impulses.

A typical man, from the moment that television was plugged in, Ryder was totally focused on it. He made no effort to hide the fact he was appalled by its size.

"That isn't a TV," he grumbled. He moved his chair to within a foot of it, the snoozing baby a part of him, like a small football nestled in the crook of his arm. "Oh, wait, it is. Imported from the land of little people, the only place on earth that is known to make a seven-inch screen." He held out his hand, and Emma slapped the remote into it.

"Nine," she told him.

He turned on the TV.

"Color," he commented with faked amazement. "Quite a concession to the times, Emma. Quite a concession."

Well, at least he hadn't even noticed the hideous, pathetic effort she had made to fix her hair.

Ryder began grimly switching from channel to channel.

"You should have televisions in the rooms," he said, not lifting his eyes from the set. "Men like that. A lot."

"Actually, I know that."

He gave her a skeptical look, as if somehow she had managed to give him the impression she was the least likely person to know what men liked. A lot.

Her hidden wild child *did* know. Maybe if she had let that wicked woman out now and then, instead of trying so hard to be circumspect, Peter would still be hers.

"Well," he said, with a hint of sarcasm, "why pander to what people like, after all? Never mind good business."

Is it that clear to him, on the basis of our very short acquaintance, that business isn't exactly my strength? Should she put in television sets next year? She hated herself for even thinking it! For letting her judgment be so influenced!

"I want people to engage in the experience I offer," she said, aware she was arguing as if she was making a case before the Supreme Court. "The White Pond Inn is about old-fashioned family time. Games in the parlor. Fishing at the pond. Hikes. Reading a book in a hammock. Watching fireflies."

How wholesome. Not a hint of wild child in that!

But she might as well have spared herself the effort. She had lost his interest. He settled Tess on the long length of his thigh. The baby, her face smudged with cookies, and her hair tangles intact, sighed with contentment in her sleep. She settled onto his leg, her padded, frilly rump pointed in the air, her legs curled underneath her tummy, her cheek resting on his knee. In moments, a gentle little snore was coming from her.

Ryder's one hand rested on her back, protective, unconsciously tender. It would have made a lovely picture to go with Emma's decor, except for the fact that his other hand had a death grip on the remote control.

And then there was the unlovely scowl that deepened on his face as each channel reported the same ominous weather.

The storm was not projected to end until the early hours of morning.

Even then, roads reopening were going to

depend on highway clean-up. One channel showed a clip of a road outside Fredericton. The scene showed devastation, the road completely blocked by sagging power lines, by trees broken and splintered by the weight of the ice on them.

Ryder snapped off the television. It looked to Emma as though he wanted to hurl her channel changer through the screen.

"Where were you going?" she asked wondering at his desperation to be out of here. "Is someone waiting for you tonight?"

"No," he said. "No one's waiting." It said something about his life—starkly lonely, not that anything about him invited sympathy. Except the baby sprawling along the muscled length of his upper thigh.

"Where were you going?" she asked again. Nothing about him invited her questions, either, and yet something made her ask them anyway. The truth was she wasn't going to be invisible ever again. Not even if that was safe.

"We were going to my cottage on Lake Kackaticka."

Emma frowned. She was familiar with the lake and the community of upscale cottages that surrounded it. At this time of year it was pretty much abandoned. A few year-round residents looked after the cottages, but the summer people stayed away. It was cold and dreary around the lake in the winter.

"Who goes there in the winter?"

"No one," he said, making no attempt to disguise his satisfaction.

"How long were you going for?"

He shrugged.

"The weekend?"

He shrugged again, and she suspected the truth.

"You weren't going to spend Christmas there, were you?"

"Yes, I was, not past tense, either. Yes, I am."

"Alone?"

"Not alone. Me and Tess."

"But what kind of Christmas would that be for her?"

He looked at the sleeping baby, doubt crossing those supremely confident features, but only for a moment.

"She has no idea that it is Christmas."

It was his right to parent that baby however he wanted, Emma told herself sternly. He was her guest. It really wasn't her place to argue with him. On the other hand, it wasn't as if she'd invited him here, or called down the weather personally to inconvenience him.

She didn't think pandering to his bad temper was a good idea, and besides she was committed to expressing her opinion after a year and a half of biting her tongue for Peter's convenience! And look where that had gotten her!

She'd already voiced her thoughts several times tonight, and apparently there was no stopping her now. In fact, she felt an obligation to render her opinion for the sake of Tess!

"That's the saddest thing I've ever heard," she told him.

He glared at the empty screen of the TV, then picked up the channel changer and turned the television back on, deciding it was interesting after all. "That just shows you've been sheltered up here in your fairy-tale world. You don't know the first thing about sad."

There was no point saying anything more. She could tell in the set of his jaw that he was the stubborn type who never would admit he was wrong or change his mind.

And yet there was that little ghost girl again, the one who'd been disappointed by every single Christmas, who insisted she knew everything there was to know about *sad* and how dare he insinuate otherwise?

It must have been the ghost girl who couldn't let it go.

Emma said, sharply, "You're depriving Tess of Christmas, that's not just selfish. It's mean."

The announcer on TV picked that moment to say, voice over a map covered with red lines of road closures that it would be three days before travel resumed on some of those roads.

Ryder Richardson swore under his breath.

"I suppose the baby doesn't know any better than that, either," Emma said.

"You know what? I need you to show me to my room." He stood up, not bothering to shut off the television, lifting the baby with graceful unconsciousness as he stood, tucking her sleeping head into his shoulder. To himself he said, almost musing. "It couldn't get much worse than this, could it?"

But Emma, dedicated to airing her views, wasn't letting it pass. Just this afternoon she had been a woman totally content with herself and her circumstances. Totally. And now wild-child and woman-scorned, and wholesome-experienced-innkeeper were all wrestling around inside her in a turmoil because of him, and she found she resented this intrusion on her life.

"No," she agreed coldly, "it couldn't."

But it did.

The lights flickered, dimmed, flickered again, and then the room was plunged into darkness. The television went out with a sputter, the embers from a dying fire threw weak golden light across them.

"It just got worse, didn't it?"

His voice in the darkness was a sensuous rasp that wild-child *loved.*

"Yes, it did," she said coolly.

"Do you ever get the feeling the gods are laughing at you?" he asked, not for the first time that night.

"Yes," she said sadly, "I do." Was now a good time to break the bad news to him? "The furnace is electric."

Her eyes were adjusting to the darkness. The firelight flashed gold, on the perfect planes of his face. Wild-child sighed.

It took him a moment to get what she meant.

"Are you saying the only source of heat in this falling-down old wreck is that fireplace?"

"Falling-down old wreck?" she breathed, incensed, pleased that woman-scorned was taking charge, getting the upper hand. "How *dare* you?"

It felt so good to say that! To stand up for herself! She wished she would have said that to Peter, at least once.

But no, not even when he'd told her, so sheepishly, while still making it *her* fault he and Monique had been seeing each other, what had she said?

I understand.

"Your front bell sounds broken, the door handle did come off in your hand, there's frost on the inside of the windows, and when I dropped the baby's bottle it rolled *down* the floor."

"Which means?" she asked haughtily.

"Probably your foundation is moving. The floor isn't level."

All her work on creating pure Christmas charm, and he was seeing *that?*

"Do you always focus on the negative?" she snapped. How much did it cost to fix a moving foundation, anyway?

"I do," he said without an ounce of apology, even though he followed up with, "Sorry."

"You aren't sorry," Emma breathed. "You're a miserable selfish man who is intent on spoiling Christmas not just for yourself, but for your niece and anyone else who has the misfortune to cross paths with you."

"Well, aren't you glad I won't be around to spoil it for you?" he said smoothly, completely unabashed by his behavior.

"Huh. With my record, you probably will still be around Christmas Day. Spoiling things."

Silence, the light softening something in his features, an illusion, nothing more. But when he spoke, there was something softer in his voice.

"What does that mean, with your record?"

Don't tell him, she ordered herself. *Don't.* But another part of her, weary, thought *Why not? What difference does it make?*

"It means I've never had a Christmas that wasn't spoiled. So why should this one be any different?"

Silence. She'd left herself wide open to his sarcasm, so thank God he was saying nothing.

Only when he did speak, she wished he'd chosen sarcasm.

"You've never had a good Christmas?" He seemed legitimately astounded. And legitimately sorry, for the first time. But then his customary skepticism won out. "Come on."

She remembered last year, excited as a small child, arriving at Peter's parents' home. No, not a home. A mansion. A picture out of a splendid movie. The trees on the long drive lit with white lights, every window of the house lit, she could see the enormous tree sparkling through the window.

And that had been the beginning of a Christmas that *looked* exactly like the Christmases she had dreamed as a little girl, but that *felt* like an excursion into hell.

"Have you?" she asked Ryder, tilting her chin proudly, knowing his answer. There was only one reason people hated Christmas, wasn't there? They'd given up trying to make it something it could never be.

Maybe it was time for her to surrender, too, to forget trying to change her fortunes, to abandon that little girl who wanted something so badly. Maybe it all was just an illusion. Christmas had become a corny, commercial package, a dream that no one could ever make a reality.

Maybe the truth was that it was a terrible time of year, laden with too much stress and far too many expectations. Maybe it would be a good time to plan a vacation to Hawaii. It probably would have been a whole lot easier to talk her mother into celebrating Christmas in Hawaii than it had been to convince her to come here.

A trip to Hawaii would be possible after a successful year of business. Maybe I'll give in and add televisions, after all. If the foundation doesn't collapse.

After a long time, he surprised her by saying, quietly and with obvious reluctance. "Yes, I have. Had good Christmases."

She could feel him shifting in the dancing light of the fireplace flames. He came way too close, and peered down at her.

He shifted the baby into the crook of his elbow, and with his free hand he did the oddest thing.

He touched her hair.

"We'll be out of your hair in no time," he said

solemnly, as if he had touched it only to make that point. "I won't wreck your Christmas, Emma."

She saw something desolate in his eyes, and was taken aback by the realization that he was trying to protect her from that.

"If you've had good Christmases, don't you want that for Tess?" she asked, quietly. "I had a mother who thought Christmas was a nuisance. It was awful."

And maybe it wasn't just Christmas, but parenthood in general, that her mother had found bothersome.

That's what had made Emma so eager to please, to prove somehow she was a good person. Worthy. Was she still trying to prove that? Was that what Holiday Happenings and Christmas Day Dream were really about?

She *hated* that she was questioning the purity of her motivations.

"Emma, I'm doing my best," he said quietly. "Just leave it."

But she couldn't. "And what if your best just isn't good enough?"

"Don't you think I ask myself that every day?"

She studied him, saw the torment in his face,

went from being angry with him and with herself and with Peter and her mother and the world, to feeling something far more dangerous. Empathy.

"If you've had good Christmases, why do you hate it so much now?" she asked him.

The pause was very long, as if he considered telling her something, fought with it, won.

"Emma, I'm just passing through. I'm not leaving my burdens here when I go."

He said it almost protectively, as if they would be too heavy for her to handle. He was right. They were strangers.

That was not changed by the fact he had touched her hair.

Or by the fact that he had an adorable baby.

It was not changed by the fact that they were marooned here by the storm, like shipwreck survivors on a desert island.

He had his baggage and she had hers, and he was right not to share it, to keep his boundaries high. It was a reminder of what she needed to do, as well.

"I'll find a flashlight," she said, moving away from the emotional minefield they were treading so lightly, realizing the only thing they had to share was how to get through a night without electricity.

She sighed. "If the power stays out, in very short order this room will be the only truly warm one in the house. I have a crib upstairs, and we can haul a mattress down here for you. I'll sleep on the couch."

"I hope the power is going to come back on," he said.

So do I, but the way my luck is running, I doubt it. "I'll show you where the crib is."

Moments later, Emma, holding the sleeping baby, was watching him take the crib apart. Despite her resolve that they be nothing more than strangers, she couldn't help but admire how comfortable he was with tools, the man-thing.

It had taken her the better part of an afternoon to put that crib together, studying instructions, putting A into B. He had the whole thing dismantled and downstairs in a matter of minutes.

While he was reassembling the crib, Emma went back upstairs to get a mattress off the bed in the room closest to the staircase.

"Tess didn't even know I'd moved her," he commented, coming up behind her.

"She sleeps like a log."

"I'm envious," he said. A man who carried burdens so heavy they affected his sleep?

Don't pursue it, she told herself.

"It's already chilly up here," he said.

"Well, you know these old wrecks. The insulation is in about the same shape as the foundation."

"I said I was sorry."

"No," she said firmly. "I have a tendency to be way too sensitive. I know there's lots wrong with the old place. It's foolish to love her anyway."

"What *do* you have for insulation?"

A pragmatic question. He didn't want to know anything about what she loved. She didn't blame him. She didn't want to know what he loved, either.

A lie. She did. Despite all her resolve, both wild-child and woman-scorned were supremely interested in what a man like him loved.

The baby was obvious, of course.

She stuck to her resolve and the relatively safe topic of her old house. " I found old newspapers in the walls when I redid the bathroom." She didn't mention how the tub falling through the floor had necessitated the renovation before she really had the funds to do it. "New insulation is on my to-do list."

"Big list?" he asked, conversationally.

But Emma already felt foolish enough for blurting out about her Christmases. She was saying nothing else to him that could be interpreted as self-pitying.

The insulation fell into that category. If she was going to borrow money, wouldn't that have been the sensible choice? New insulation? A new roof?

Oh, no, dreamer that she was she had been spending money on gifts for needy families, and redoing this bedroom in preparation for her mother's visit.

Was she still trying to prove herself worthy? Emma shut the thought off fast and focused on problems she could solve.

If she didn't become more prudent, next year she would probably be heading the "needy" line, not jetting off to Hawaii!

She had gambled everything on the success of Holiday Happenings. How many days of her Christmas moneymaker could she lose before she was in real trouble?

"Oh," she said, breezily, not letting any of

those concerns leach into her voice, "it's a big list, but nothing I can't handle."

She was trying to regain ground as a complete professional.

They were in the room at the top of the steps that she called the green room. Once it had been her grandmother's, stuffed from top to bottom with clutter, a dusty-rose wall-to-wall carpet covering the beautiful aged hardwoods.

Now, in preparation for her mother's arrival, it was the most beautiful room in the house. The carpet had been ripped out, the faded layers of wallpaper stripped. The room had been restored to historical correctness and decorated in her mother's favorite color. It was her loveliest room, and Emma felt it not only showcased her abilities as a competent and professional innkeeper, but would convince her mother that White Pond was not such a bad place.

And that her daughter isn't such a bad person?

Where were these thoughts coming from? Still, she glanced at Ryder to see if he was suitably impressed, and saw he was looking at a huge crack in the wall that was opening above the window. That figured.

She really didn't want to hear what *that* meant, so she directed the flashlight beam to the focal point of the room, a beautiful antique four-poster with a lace canopy, layered with luxurious silk bedding and pillows in subtle shades of green.

"Nice piece of furniture," he said. Trying to gain ground for his "old-wreck" remark? Not wanting to let her know what the crack meant, either? Feeling sorry for her because she had never had a good Christmas?

She had shown dozens of guests to their rooms and never felt like this before.

As if the bed was a strangely intimate piece of furniture, and she was tempting something to be in here alone with him.

"It's not really a nice piece of furniture," she said, trying to sound as if she was not strangling. "The first night I put guests in it, it broke."

She had meant it to sound funny but it sounded pathetic, lost her any ground she had gained at presenting herself as a competent professional. Instead, she felt her own failing.

But he didn't notice. "Hmm. That sounds interesting. What were they doing?"

That strangling sound in her throat intensified.

She refused to answer him or even look at him. Wild-child had a few ideas about what they might have been doing, but Emma was ignoring wild-child. She redirected the flashlight beam and hurried to the bed.

"Do you think we can just leave it made up?" She didn't wait for her answer, lifted a corner of the mattress, struggled to swing it off the bed frame and retain her grip on the flashlight.

"Stop it," he said. "You take the bedding and light the way for me. I'll get the mattress."

"I can clearly see if I let you get away with bossing me around once, you'll turn into a complete horror."

"As if I'm not already," he muttered. "Emma, I'm being reasonable. The mattress is too big for you."

"You are looking at a woman who refinished every inch of flooring in this place by herself. I've knocked down walls. I've repaired plumbing. I've been up on the roof. I've—" *failed to pay the bills, failed to impress my mother, lost my fiancé over this place...*

He held up his hand before she could rush on with her list. "Stop," he said dryly. "I'm having a heart attack thinking about it." But he was obviously thinking about it, because that familiar scowl creased his brow. "I hope you didn't put those Christmas lights on the peak of the roof yourself."

Tim had already given her a very thorough lecture about that. She wasn't listening to another one.

"I'm just making the point—I can handle my end of the mattress." She turned the flashlight beam on the floor so he couldn't see her face, which was blushing as if she had said something about sex. *Couldn't I have worded that differently?*

"Why do I have a feeling that what you think you can handle and what you really can handle are two entirely different things?"

"Because you're a chauvinist pig?" she asked, keeping her voice deliberately sweet, glad he couldn't see her face because his statement could sum up her knowledge of sex, too.

"Gee, and a minute ago I was worried you were going to fall down the steps and have the mattress and me land on top of you. Now I'm thinking if you fell, could you at least bite your tongue? Preferably off."

"You charmer, you."

Was a desert-island camaraderie developing between them? Wild-child was jumping up and down at the desert-island possibilities.

"At least let me take the end that's going down the stairs first."

"No," she said stubbornly. Woman-scorned, who didn't need a man taking charge of anything, took over. She picked up the foot of the mattress and began dragging it along the floor, leaving him with no choice but to pick up the other end. She was trying not to grunt as they headed for the stairs, but the mattress was an awkward bundle, hard to get a grip on, heavier than she had thought it would be.

As it turned out, he'd been right about the bedding, too. They should have made two separate trips. Because as they neared the middle of the stairway, the silk caught in the holly on the railing.

She paused to untangle it before it pulled the whole garland down or tore the silk. She dropped the flashlight, and they were in darkness.

It happened fast after that.

"Wait a sec—" she cried as she felt the mattress

pressing against her. But it was too late. The mattress squeezed by her, sweeping her along with it. Emma grabbed a fistful of something before being plunged downward into complete darkness.

CHAPTER FOUR

"ARE you okay?" Ryder called.

Emma couldn't answer at first, the wind knocked temporarily out of her.

"Are you hurt?" he asked again. She could hear him trying to get past the mattress that blocked the stairs.

"Fine," she managed to get out before he made a hole in the wall, bumping against it like that. The walls were admittedly flimsy in an "old wreck" of a house like this.

She couldn't help it. Emma began to giggle and then to laugh. But he mistook the muffled howls of her laughter for cries of pain and came hurtling down to her. Predictably, he got caught up where the mattress blocked the step, and he crashed down on it beside her.

They lay there, side by side, on the mattress

that blocked the staircase. Their legs and feet were up the stairs, their heads and backs on the floor of the foyer. They were only faintly illuminated by the shadows the firelight in the next room was throwing against the wall.

The laughter died in her throat as Emma became aware of how solid he felt beside her, how his presence here in the house during the storm was somehow reassuring.

Even if he was an ass who thought her house was a wreck and who was going to deprive Tess of Christmas.

"Emma, are you okay?"

"I'm fine," she assured him again, though as she drank in the scent of him she wondered how true that was. "Are you?"

She felt him get up on his elbow, stare through darkness made only a little less black by the slight light leaching in from the other room.

He lay back down, sighed. "I guess I'm okay. Providing jest for the gods tonight. So, did one of your spirits push you down the stairs?"

"Oh, no, just made sure the mattress was there when I hit the floor."

"Ah."

Was his cynicism slightly tempered? Ryder had altered his position slightly, and Emma could feel the solidness of his shoulder touching hers, make out the strong line of his nose, the sensuous curve of his mouth.

"I want you to know I'm not the kind of girl who ends up on a mattress with a guy on such a short acquaintance," she teased, trying to reduce with humor the tension she felt in her belly.

"I already guessed," he said softly.

And her humor left her. What did that mean?

"Remember when I said I didn't think things could get any worse?" Ryder asked softly.

"Yes?"

"Around you they can. And they do."

"I know," she agreed, "The White Christmas curse."

"Maybe it's not a curse," he said softly. "Maybe it's magic, just like you said. And I'm not sure which I'm more afraid of."

And then he was laughing. It was a rusty sound, self-deprecating and reluctant, as if he had not laughed for a long, long time and did not particularly want to laugh now.

For all that, it was a sound so lovely, so richly

masculine and so genuine, that it made her want to stay in this place, on a mattress jammed half on the stairs and half off, with this man beside her for as long as she could, to rest a moment in this place that was as real as any place she had ever been before.

Woman-scorned *tsked* disapprovingly.

Well, why not laugh, Ryder thought? His situation was absurd. He was trapped at a place dedicated to Christmas corniness, the power was out, the storm raged on. He could hear it rattling the windows and hounding the eaves. He was lying in the pitch darkness on a crashed mattress, with Emma so close to him he could smell the scent of lavender on her skin.

Life was playing a cosmic joke on him, why not laugh?

Why keep fighting this? He was stuck, she was stuck, they were in this together, whether he liked it or not. The powerful surge of intensity he was feeling toward her was only because of the crisis nature of the situation. People in situations like this tended to bond to each other in way too short a time.

He could not act on that. Maturity was being required of him. A certain amount of cooperation was going to be needed to get them through this, but nothing more.

There was no sense railing against the unfairness of life. He'd already done that, and it made no difference. It never changed what was, it only made the experience more miserable than it had to be.

"I'm sorry," she said, her voice still light with laughter. "I should have listened to you. I should have taken the bedding off, let you take the mattress, followed meekly behind—"

"Oh, yeah," he said, "I can certainly picture you in the meek position. Submissive, even. Would that be before or after you strung lights on the roofline and knocked out a wall or two?"

"Hmm," she said, pretending thoughtfulness. "Let's make it before. I might be too tired after to be properly meek."

Then they were laughing again, and he noticed her laughter was sweet, uncomplicated, real, like when Tess laughed.

"I'm sorry, too," he said, finally, "for taking out my frustration at having my plans interrupted on you. And for calling your house an old wreck. It isn't really. It's a Victorian, probably built at the very end of the eighteen-hundreds or in the early nineteen-hundreds."

"How do you know that?"

"I'm an architect. Though I have to admit, I avoid old-house projects like the plague. People are never realistic about what it's going to cost to restore an old building."

"Don't you think old buildings are romantic?" she asked.

Given the startling intensity between them, he did not want to discuss anything about romance with her.

"Not at all," he said. "You get in and the walls aren't square, the floors aren't level, the fifty-year-old addition is being held up by toothpicks. I prefer new construction, and my real prefer-ence is commercial buildings."

She was silent for a bit, and he hoped she was contemplating getting out of this old place before it ruined her financially, but naturally that wasn't what she was contemplating at all.

"We could start over," she decided.

"Could we? How?"

"Like this." Her hand found his in the darkness. And shook it. "Hi," she said, "I'm Emma White, the meek, submissive owner of the White Christmas Inn."

Her hand was soft in his, and again he felt something when he touched her that went beyond the sizzle of chemistry. Quiet strength. He turned his head to see her in the faint shadows being cast by the fireplace in the other room.

"I'm Ryder Richardson," he played along, despite the fact he knew this was a somewhat dangerous game, that he was incredibly aware of the loveliness of her hand and her scent.

Still, he was reluctantly amazed by how good it felt to play along with her, to let go of his legendary self-control, just a little bit.

She was silent for a while. "Do you think," she said hesitantly, "just in this new spirit of cooperation, you could tell me what a really good Christmas feels like? You said you'd had good Christmases. Just so I know exactly what to do for the Christmas Day Dream."

She was moving him further and further behind enemy lines.

"Come on," he said, "you have some good Christmas memories."

Her silence nearly took what was left of his heart.

Ryder was amazed to find his carefully walled world had a hole in it that she had crept through. He was amazed that he *wanted* to go there, to a good, good Christmas, to share it with her, to make it real for her, but for himself, too. To relive such a wonderful time proved to be a temptation too strong to resist, even as he wondered if he was going to regret this later.

"You wouldn't think this would be the best Christmas ever," he said, slowly, feeling his way cautiously through the territory that had once been his life, "but when I was twelve my dad was out of work, the only time I ever remember that happening while I was growing up."

He told her about how his dad and his mom had snuck out every night into the backyard and shoveled and leveled and sprayed the garden hose on sub-zero nights until they had a perfect ice rink to unveil to him and Drew on Christmas morning.

He and his brother had woken up to second-hand skates that didn't fit, and instead of turkey they'd had a bonfire in the backyard and cooked smokies and marshmallows.

They had skated all day. Pretty soon all the neighbors had drifted over, the neighborhood boys unanimously voting the Richardson brothers' skating rink as the best gift of the year. At midnight there had still been people around the bonfire, kids skating, babies sleeping.

"And then, our neighbor Mrs. Kelly, who sang solos at all the community weddings and funerals started singing 'Silent Night,' and everybody gathered at the bonfire and started singing, too." Ryder's parents had been dead now for more than a dozen years, but as he talked about them, he could feel their love for him and Drew as if it had all happened yesterday.

Maybe she had been right about ghosts living here. His parents had always been determined to make the best of everything. *Life gives you lemons, you make lemonade,* his mother had always said. He wondered what they would think of him, and how he was coping with the lemons life had handed him.

And suddenly reliving that memory didn't feel

fun anymore and already he felt regret, and felt the shadows pulling at him, trying to take him back.

Fast forward to spending last Christmas Eve with Drew and Tracy, opening his gift from them. A gag gift, as always, a huge stuffed marlin, possibly the ugliest thing Ryder had ever seen, mocking the deep-sea fishing trip he and Drew had taken off the coast of Mexico earlier in the year. Was that the last time he had laughed, really laughed, until tonight?

Come on, stay, his brother had said, at the door, "Silent Night" playing on the stereo inside the house. *We'll put you in the guest room. You can watch Tess open her presents tomorrow.*

Since Tess had been a cute and occasionally smelly little lump of a person at the time, incapable of opening her own presents, and probably oblivious to what they contained, Ryder had failed to see the attraction of that. He could clearly see the baby was going to have no appreciation whatsoever for the signed football he had gotten for her.

But he had stayed, something about the magic of family being stronger than any other kind of magic.

It was the last night he had ever experienced joy. It was the last time he had laughed. Until tonight.

And he did not feel ready to invite those kinds of experiences into his life again. He had built his barricades for a reason—he was not nearly done beating himself up for his failure to save them all. But also to keep this out: longing for what could not be, ever again.

A man had to be whole, unencumbered, to welcome experiences like those into his life. He was not that man. The easygoing young man he had been only a year ago was scarred beyond recognition.

And knew he would not be that man again.

Emma seemed to sense his mood shifting, changing, even though she could barely see him. He let go of her hand abruptly. She felt the faint tensing, his energy drawing away from her. She tried to draw him back.

"Would you like to hear about Christmas at the inn?"

He wanted to tell her no, to grab back the things he had just told her, but that seemed too sour, even for him, and it seemed to be going against the new spirit of cooperation he had promised, so he grunted instead.

She took the grunt as interest, and she told him about Holiday Happenings and her neighbors helping her get ready, about the skating and the sleigh-riding, the craft sales, the wreaths, the amount of food they hoped to sell.

"I hope it's as wonderful as the night you just described to me," she said, "if it happens. What am I going to do with four thousand hot dogs if it doesn't?"

"Four thousand?"

"I always think big," she said ruefully. "I was thinking if a hundred people showed up every night for ten days and each ate two hot dogs, I would need two thousand. And then I started thinking, what if two hundred people showed up every night? Or what if a hundred and fifty showed up, but a few of them were teenage boys?"

Her math and her hopeless optimism were giving him a headache. Or maybe that was the thinly disguised worry in her voice.

"You already bought everything?" he asked. Despite the fact he'd commanded himself not to encourage her with interest, to stop this, he hated that she'd apparently invested more than she could afford to lose in singlehandedly bringing the Christmas spirit to Willowbrook.

Now, no one was coming.

At least not tonight. "You still have nine days to recoup your losses," he said. But he wasn't sure if he believed it. What if the storm lasted longer, or if it was like 1998 and the Atlantic seaboard was shut down for days? What if the power didn't come back on for weeks?

Just because he was stranded here with her, lying on a mattress with her, that didn't make it his problem.

He didn't care. No, that wasn't the whole truth. He didn't *want* to care.

"Where are the hot dogs now?" he asked reluctantly.

"Freezer."

"If the power doesn't come on by tomorrow, you could put them in a snowbank."

She said nothing.

"It'll be okay," he said. Hey, he'd get home and send her a check to cover her hot dogs.

"It *has* to be," she said, and he didn't like what

he heard in her voice one little bit. As if her whole life depended on Holiday Happenings working out.

"What do you mean it *has* to be?" Ryder knew from experience you had to be careful about throwing challenges like that at fate. It had a way of never giving people what they thought they wanted.

She told him about inviting the needy families, the gifts under the tree, the perfect Christmas Day she had planned for them.

He could feel himself closing his eyes, trying to steel himself against her *goodness*.

Suddenly she went silent. "Look at me chattering on and on," she said, embarrassed, probably figuring out that being stranded gave the illusion of camaraderie, but it didn't really make him worthy of hearing her dreams, sharing her confidences.

Why had he allowed himself to be sucked into this?

Not just alone, a voice answered him, *lonely*.

He hated that admission, the weakness of it. He had failed his brother and his sister-in-law. He *deserved* to feel the way he felt.

Still, something in him that was still human said to her, and meant it, "It's good that you believe."

There was that word again, creeping around the edges of his life, looking for a way to sneak past his guard and into his heart.

So it would be ready to break again.

I don't think so, he said to himself.

"Oh," she said, and laughed self-consciously. "I didn't mean to sound like that. Saint Emma."

"Don't forget—of the meek and submissive school of saints." Giving in, just a little bit, to that temptation to play with her.

But giving in a little bit was probably just a forerunner to giving in a lot. And in the end she was going to get hurt. He needed to pull back from this *now,* not just to protect himself. To protect her.

He got to his feet, hesitated, and then reached back a hand for her when the mattress was thwarting her efforts to get up. The momentum of that tug pulled her into the length of him. He could feel her slightness, her softness, the delicious hint of curves. The enveloping lavender scent of her that would make it so easy to lose his head.

The devil told him not to bother being a better

man, not to bother protecting her. It told him to outrun the terrible loneliness reliving his memories had stirred up inside him.

She was an adult. Kiss her. See what happened.

He could almost taste her lips when he thought of that. A wanting, compelling, tempting, tantalizing, swept through him.

More than a year since he had connected with another human being.

But not her, he told himself sternly. You could not kiss a girl like Emma White without thinking it all the way through. Following an impulse could have far-reaching ramifications.

Emma wanted to be fiercely independent, knocking down walls and climbing all over the roof by herself. She wanted to send the message, *I don't need a man.*

But she struck him, with her Christmas fantasies, with her wistfulness, with her desire to bring something to others, as not just old-fashioned and decent, but romantic. Emma was the type of woman who might think a casual kiss meant things it did not mean. She might think that he wanted to get to know her better or was looking for a mommy for little Tess, a future that involved her.

The truth was Ryder Richardson did not look to the future at all.

Ryder just got through every day to the best of his ability. And that, he told himself sternly, did not involve doing damage to others. And how could he not damage someone like her? *Vinegar and milk,* he reminded himself.

"I'll get the mattress pulled into the great room, if you want to go find some bedding to make up the couch."

"Yes, boss," she said.

The temptation rose again. To play along with her. But this time he said nothing in response to her jesting.

In fact, he made up his mind he was leaving at first light.

You'd leave a woman alone with no power? a voice inside him asked.

For her own good, he answered it back.

But maybe she had been closer to the truth than he wanted to admit when she had called him mean and selfish.

It was himself he was protecting, not her.

Protecting himself from these uncomfortable feelings, something thawing in him that allowed him to see his world as too stark, too masculine. Too lonely.

But getting to know someone was a minefield that rarely went smoothly, especially now that he carried so much baggage, so many scars, so much damage.

What started with a curious kiss could all blow up and leave her with another Christmas in shambles.

Not one good Christmas memory? How was that possible? And yet he could tell she was honest to a fault, and that if she could have dredged one up, she would have.

He dragged the mattress into the living room, rearranged the bedding, stoked the fire. The thought of sharing this room with her for the night seemed uncomfortably intimate given his vow not to encourage anything between them.

She came back down the stairs, loaded down with bedding, the duvet a plump eiderdown, whiter than a wedding night and just as sensual.

"Where's the woodpile?" he asked, looking

everywhere but at her lips, needing a moment's breathing space.

She told him, and he put on his shoes and grabbed the flashlight. He went out the back door into the storm to her woodshed. The night, bitter and dark, the flashlight beam, frail against the wicked slant of white sleet, were in sharp contrast to the cozy intimacy inside, but Ryder welcomed the wind, the sharded sleet on his face slapping him back to reality. The sleet was freezing as it hit the ground, forcing him to focus intensely to keep upright, especially once his arms were loaded with wood.

He made five or six trips to the shed, filling the wood box beside the fireplace. Each time he came in, he would think *enough,* but the picture Emma made cuddled up on the couch inside her quilt, her hair every which way, would make him think *not one good Christmas,* as if he could or should do something about it. And that would send him back out the door, determined to cling to his vision of life as a cold and bitter place.

But going out into the weather again and again turned out to be one of those impulses he should have thought all the way through.

His clothes were soaked. He made one more trip—out to his vehicle, to bring in the luggage he had not wanted to bring in. *Another surrender,* he thought, shivering. The old house only had one bathroom, upstairs, and it was already cold. He noticed the tub seemed new, and the flooring around it did, too. He inspected more closely.

Her tub had fallen through the floor at some point in recent history. This place was way too much for her, and he killed the fleeting thought that she needed someone to help her. He hurried into a pair of drawstring plaid pajama pants, a T-shirt.

When he came back down, he noticed she was in pajamas now, too, soft pink, with white-and-pink angels on them, flannel, not, thankfully, the least bit sexy. Her blanket was a soft mound of snow on the couch, but she was up doing something at the fire.

He saw then that she was pouring steaming water from a huge cast-iron kettle she had put in the coals of the fire. She came to him with a mug of hot chocolate.

It was just a little too much like a pajama party, and he had talked enough for one night. Yet

chilled to the bone because of his own foolishness, he could not refuse. He took the mug,
wrapped his hands around its comforting heat.
He took a chair across from her as she snuggled
back under her blanket, one hand coming out of
the folds to hold her hot chocolate.

Home.

The scene, straight out of a magazine layout
for Christmas, had a feeling of home about it:
fire crackling, baby sleeping, the pajamas, the
hot chocolate, the tree in the background.

"Is it hard?" she asked softly. "Looking after
Tess? How long have you done it for?"

That was the problem with letting his guard
down, telling the one story. For a whole year he
had avoided any relationship that required
anything of him, even conversation. It was just
too hard to make small talk, to pretend to care.
Being engaged with another human being felt
exhausting and like a lie.

His failure had killed his brother. Hardly a
conversation starter, and yet how long could he
know someone before he felt compelled to tell
them that? Because that had become the biggest
part of him.

But now that he had confided one deeply personal memory to her, it was as if a hole had opened in the dam that held his loneliness, and the words wanted to pour out of him.

"I was appointed her guardian three months ago." Ryder did not want to tell her the circumstances, Tracy's long fight ending, nor did he want to tell her how hard those first weeks had been. Thinking about them, loneliness and longing threatened to swamp him again.

But his voice was carefully neutral when he said, "I have a nanny. That helps. She's an older lady, married, her own kids grown up. She misses children." So much easier to talk about Mrs. Markle than himself.

But Emma persisted. "And when she's not there?"

"There's the hair thing," he admitted. "I do pretty good at everything else. The first few diaper changes I felt like I was scaling Everest without oxygen, but now it makes me feel oddly manly. Like I look at other guys and think, *I can handle stuff you can't even imagine, pal.*" He was still aware he was hiding in humor, but Emma's appreciative chuckle made it seem like a good tactic, so he kept going.

"Shopping for her is a nightmare. It's like being at a pigeon convention. You've never heard so much cooing. It's like I'm transformed from six-foot-one of highly-muscled, menacing man to this adorable somewhat helpless teddy bear."

"You do have kind of a menacing air about you, Ryder." Her eyes slid to his arms to check out the muscle part. He was pretty sure she wasn't disappointed. The gym was one of the places where he took it all, sweated it out, pushed himself to a place beyond thought.

"A much-needed defense against cooing, not that it works in the baby store. I go in for a new supply of pajamas with feet in them, the entire extent of Tess's wardrobe, and women come out of the woodwork. I get shown little diaper covers with frills and bows on them, and white dresses that Tess would destroy in thirty seconds flat, and the worst thing of all—hair paraphernalia."

"I noticed you bought the little diaper cover."

"I know," he admitted. "I get the hair junk, too, and more ridiculous shoes than you can shake a stick at, too."

"Ah, the boots with the penguins."

"I learned to just let them load me up, and I can get out of there quicker."

"Maybe underneath the menace, they see something else."

He could tell her. He could tell this stranger about his last year in hell, leave his burdens here when he walked away. It was pushing away at the damaged dam within him, wanting out.

Instead he said, coolly, "Something else? Not that I'm aware of."

"Hmm," she said with patent disbelief. He bet if he met up with her in the baby department, she'd be cooing along with the rest of them.

"Maybe they see a man doing his best in a difficult situation. Maybe they admire the fact you said yes to being put in that situation."

"It's not like I had a choice."

"I bet you did," she said.

"Not really."

"No, because a man like you would only see the right choice, and never even realize there was another one."

He snorted. "You don't know me well enough to say that." But another voice, Tracy telling him the night before she married his brother, *You and Drew are the rarest of finds. Good men.*

That was before he had failed his brother and her.

Was there anything left of a good man in him? If there was, why would he even consider leaving Emma here, alone, a woman without power?

Self-preservation.

"You must have had the choice to walk away," Emma said. "I think when you hold that baby, you can't hide who you really are. That's what makes you irresistible—"

He looked into her eyes for a moment, almost felt his heart stop beating. If she found him irresistible they were both in deep trouble.

But she finished her sentence, "—in the baby department."

He felt his heart start beating again, but was warily aware his reaction to how she had finished that sentence was mixed. Part relief, more regret.

He was not sure he liked the way this was going, because if she prodded him now, he had the horrible feeling he would spill all, tell all. He had done enough spilling for one night.

He gulped down the hot chocolate, set it on the table beside him, got up and stretched deliberately.

"I'm done in," he said, much more polite than saying I'm done talking, since he'd made a mental agreement with himself to have a truce with her.

Emma said, "Quit fighting it."

For a horrible moment he thought she had read his mind, seen his weakness, but instead, she said, "Go to bed, Ryder."

It would have been much less awkward if bed wasn't right there in front of her, but it was what it was. He crawled in between the sheets of his mattress on the floor and was amazed by how comfortable the bed was, how strangely content he felt despite the restless directions his thoughts had taken tonight.

He kept his eyes closed as he heard her settling on the couch, discouraging himself from looking at her and feeling those unwanted desires.

A desire to connect with another human being.

One over the age of two.

Ha, he told himself sternly. He would be ready to reconnect when pigs flew.

"Good night, Ryder," she said softly. "Sleep well. I'm glad you're here."

Was she feeling the illusion of home, too? Despite all her proclamations of independence was she feeling safer having a man in the house with that storm raging outside and no power?

But then she added sleepily, "I would hate to think of you and Tess out in that storm somewhere."

He didn't rationalize with her, didn't point out to her if they were out in that storm somewhere they wouldn't be here. She would not even have known they existed.

Instead he thought about it: she was glad they were here *for them,* not for herself. And she was putting on this big Christmas event for others, not for herself.

Who was doing anything for her this Christmas? The homeless and the needy were coming here, what about her own family? Was she as alone as he was?

"You're not going to be alone, are you?" he asked, even though he had ordered himself not to. "On Christmas?"

"I told you. Fifty-one confirmed guests."

He heard something, knew she was holding back.

"A guest isn't family," he said.

"And my mother is coming."

"That's good." He wanted to probe something, an uncertainty, he'd heard in her voice, but that was enough of tangling his life with hers.

Troubled by those thoughts, way too aware of her proximity and the soft puffs of her breath as she fell asleep, he finally surrendered, too. But he slept like a cat, alert, one eye open, gauging the fire and the storm noises outside.

Finally, relieved, Ryder noticed gray light seeping into the room through the heavy closed drapes. Morning at last. The fire was embers again, and he could tell by the chill in the room the power was still not on.

He sat up and checked the baby, still asleep.

And then his eyes drifted to Emma. She was wrapped up like a sausage in the feather duvet she had brought down from upstairs, her dark hair sticking up in sharp contrast to it.

In her sleep, her brow was deeply furrowed, as if she could not let go of some pressing worry—probably hot dogs, or bathtubs falling through the floor—and Ryder could feel the concern for her aloneness. The sloping kitchen floor and that crack above the window in that room upstairs meant something was going on with the foundation. The door chime hadn't sounded right, either, and could be an indication of a bigger problem somewhere. This place was obviously too much for her, even before Holiday Happenings—and try as he might he couldn't quite shrug it off.

Sometime during the night he had cemented his decision to leave here.

Because he had laughed.

Because he had given in, ever so briefly, to the temptation to be a different man. Because you could begin to care about a woman like Emma even if you didn't want to.

Because he had hoped for something when the word *irresistible* had tumbled so easily off her lips, and despite the fact she had clarified what she meant, those mist-and-moss eyes had said something else.

He got up quietly, added wood to the fire, went to the window and lifted the drape. For the first time he noticed the difference from last night. It was quiet, now, eerily so, no wind. He noticed the snow and rain had stopped and the horizon was tinged with the indigo blue of a clear day. In the growing light he could see broken branches littering her front yard. A huge limb had missed his vehicle by inches.

The trees dripped blue ice, and the power line coming up to her yard was nearly on the ground it was so heavy with the rain that had frozen on it.

But the storm was over.

He had to go. But where, with all the roads closed?

Anywhere.

Other travelers had to be stranded. Churches were probably offering temporary shelter, recreation centers. Roads never stayed closed for long. He was sure they would reopen today, probably within hours now that the storm was over.

He went into her kitchen, the floor freezing on his bare feet, but he opened drawers until he found a screwdriver. He was fixing the front-door handle when Emma woke up.

"Morning."

He turned and looked at Emma. She was stretching, her hair sticking straight up.

She pulled back the duvet she had slept under,

he could see the pajamas, pink flannel, little pink-and-white angels on them.

"The storm's over," he told her.

She cocked her head, listened. "Ah," she said, "the sweet sensation of survival."

"Your yard is a mess."

She came and stood beside him, surveyed the destruction being revealed by the growing morning light. Her shoulders drooped. "The pond probably looks the same way. How am I going to get that cleaned up for Holiday Happenings?"

"I don't know," he said.

She looked annoyed. "I was talking to myself, not expecting you to volunteer. And you don't have to fix the door, either." She made a grab for the screwdriver, but he held it away from her.

"If you could refill that kettle and put it on the fire, I can heat something up for the baby. Not to mention get a coffee into you. Sheesh. Prickly."

She turned from him abruptly, and then Ryder noticed it wasn't angels on her pajamas at all.

Pigs flying.

And then the baby screamed. Not her normal

wakeup crabby cry but an animal shriek of pain and panic.

He set down the screwdriver and raced back into the great room, frightened that Tess had tried to climb out of her crib and had fallen.

But she stood at the side of her crib, screaming and jumping up and down, fixated on the fire.

He went and scooped her up, tucked her in tight to his shoulder, swayed with her.

"Shhh, baby," he said, and then not knowing where the words came from, only that he needed to say whatever would bring her comfort, he said, "Shhh. Mama's here."

And for a man who did not believe such things, he did feel as though Tracy was there, in some way, helping him soothe the baby, because Tess quieted against his shoulder, but refused to be put down, and would not even look in the direction of the fireplace.

Would a more sensitive person have realized the fire was going to traumatize the baby?

He felt the burden of his inadequacy, and then he realized Emma was watching him, a tender little smile on her lips and tiny tears sparkling in her eyes.

"I'm leaving," he said, before she admired him too much, before he became like a junkie, unable to live without that look on her face.

It was a look that erased his insecurities about not being sensitive and not being good with hair, a look that said, as clearly as if Emma had spoken, that she thought he was enough.

He rested in that for a moment, in the relief that someone thought he was enough for this child.

But then he steeled himself, reminded himself Emma did not know the whole story, and said again, more firmly than before. "I'm leaving."

CHAPTER FIVE

RYDER told himself he wasn't just being mean
and selfish, either. Tess was terrified of the fireplace and the fire within it, her tiny body trembling against his chest, her fist wrapped in his
shirt so he couldn't get away from her.

He couldn't stay here with her. Even now, he
was being very careful to use his body as a
shield, placing it between Tess and the fire.

"Is Tess okay?" Emma asked. "What happened?"

"The fire scared her."

Thankfully, Emma accepted that explanation
without asking him to elaborate. Her eyes went
to the window where he'd opened the drape.
Sunshine was beginning to spackle the walls.

"Is that wise? To leave? You should at least
wait to hear what condition the roads are in.
They could still be closed."

She had no electricity. He wasn't going to "hear" anything here. But he could tell it was not a rational explanation that she wanted.

Trying to take the screwdriver from him had been a token effort. Emma wanted him to stay, as if she had already formed some kind of attachment to the man who could least be trusted with attachments.

"The roads are never closed for long," Ryder said. Hopefully. The 1998 ice storm had been called the storm of the century for a reason: such storms happened once a century.

Of course, it was a new century now, and so far his luck had been abysmal.

"It's not as if you have urgent business," Emma said, and that furrow in her brow deepened as she turned worried eyes to the baby. "Your cottage isn't going anywhere."

But, of course, he did have urgent business. He had to reclaim the bastions that had had cracks knocked into them last night, he had to repair that hole in the wall she had slipped through. Even repaired, it would be a weak place now, and she knew where it was. If he stayed, she might slip through it again.

"I appreciate the shelter from the storm, Emma."

He appreciated more than that: the refuge, for a moment when he had laughed, and for another when he had remembered Christmas past, from the storms within himself, the glimpse of what it would be to be a different man, to have that feeling of home again.

But he wasn't ready and there was a possibility he never would be. People could only get hurt if he tried.

"We've imposed long enough."

She looked as though she had something to say about that, but she bit her lip instead.

"If you'll provide me with a bill, I'll finish getting Tess ready. I don't suppose you accept credit cards?"

Breaking it down to a business deal. Reminding her it was a business deal. Despite the mattress thing. Despite him sharing a memory with her of a long-ago Christmas that shone in his memory. Magic.

Despite knowing she had never had a good Christmas.

She looked insulted. "I'm not taking money! Hot dogs for supper and a bed on the floor! No, consider your stay at the White Christmas Inn my gift to you, humble as it was."

Ryder didn't want to accept a gift from her. He hated it that she was offering one. Was she intent on giving that Christmas spirit to everyone, even those completely undeserving? Who would not make Santa's *nice* list?

But she had that mulish look on her face, and he wasn't going to argue. He'd mail her a check when he got home after Christmas. No, an anonymous money order because she'd probably be stubborn enough not to cash a check with his name on it.

Even if by after Christmas she'd mortgaged the place to pay for her hot dogs, and her falling-down house, and her fantasy Christmas day for the needy.

So, he'd make sure it was a darn generous check.

"Speaking of hot dogs," he said. "Don't forget, if the power stays out much longer, you'll have to take them out of the freezer."

What a hero, Ryder told himself cynically, *leaving her without power, but making sure to dispense hot-dog-saving advice before departing.*

A sound broke the absolute silence of the

morning, a high-pitched whining engine noise.
A snowmobile.

It was now full light out. The landscape
outside the inn looked like a broken fairy tale,
trees smashed, lines dangling, but everything
coated in a thin shimmering sheet of incredibly
beautiful blue-diamond ice.

A snowmobile pulling a sled came around the
corner of the house. A man drove the snow
machine; the sled had a woman and two little
girls in it

"My neighbors," Emma said, and a smile of
pure delight lit her face. "The Fenshaws. That's
Tim driving, his daughter-in-law, Mona, and his
two granddaughters, Sue and Peggy."

Relief washed over Ryder. She wouldn't be
alone, after all. She had people who cared about
her. Cared about her enough to be here at first
light making sure she was all right.

He was free to leave.

The Fenshaws didn't so much come into the
house as tumble in, laden with thermoses and
a huge basket wafting the incredible smell of
homemade bread. Flurried introductions
were made.

The girls, perhaps nine and eleven, spotted Tess and put the baskets they were carrying down.

"A baby," they breathed in one voice.

The older one, Sue, came and took Tess from him with surprising expertise, put her on her hip, danced across the foyer to her mother.

"Look, Mom. Isn't she the cutest thing ever? Oh, I can't wait to comb her hair!"

As tempting as it would be to stay for that, and to sample whatever was in those baskets, now would be the perfect time to make his getaway, leaving Emma amongst all this energy and love.

"Actually, Tess and I were just getting ready to leave," Ryder said, amazed by his own reluctance, knowing, though, that that very reluctance was telling him it was time to go. He had to bite his tongue to keep himself from reminding her about the hot dogs again.

"Were you now?"

The man, Tim, weathered face and white hair, was kicking off his boots inside the front door. He rounded on Ryder and eyed him, taking in the pajamas and the mattress on the floor in the other room in one sweep of his gaze which was deeply and protectively suspicious.

"We got stranded by the storm," Ryder said, pleased by the older man's suspicion rather than put out by it. He was happy Emma had someone this fiercely protective of her, someone to look out for her. It relieved him of a burden he had taken on without wanting to. "But we're leaving now."

Tim had one of those faces Ryder could read. Loss was etched there, and yet calm, too, as if Tim had made peace with what was, didn't even consider asking the world to take back its unfairness and cruelties.

"You think I'd arrive on my snowmobile if the driveway was open?" the man said. "Trees all over the thing."

Ryder stared at him. He'd been so anxious to go he had not seen what was right in front of him.

"You better have yourself some grub, son, and then we got us some work to do. You look like a city boy. You know how to run a chain saw?"

Ryder wanted to protest being called son. He wanted to rail against fate keeping him here when he was desperate to get out.

"We'll eat in the living room," Mona said, as if it was all decided. "It'll be too cold in the rest of the house."

"Tess doesn't like the living room."

But he was ignored and Tess, clearly enamored of the little girls, only cast a suspicious look at the fireplace before taking her cue from the other children and allowing herself to be put in the place of honor at the very center of the picnic blanket they were laying out on the floor.

The basket was unpacked, and soon they were tucking into homemade bread and jam, steaming mugs of coffee.

The magic seemed to be deepening in this place, as the two little girls fussed over Tess... and over him.

"This is my doll," Peggy told him, wagging a worn rag doll in his face. "Her name is Bebo."

"Uh, that's an unusual name."

"Do you think it's pretty?"

It rated up there with *Holiday Happenings* on his ugly-name list, but he couldn't look into that earnest face and say that. Considering it practice for when Tess would be asking him such difficult questions, he said, "I think it's very creative."

Peggy frowned at him, not fooled. "I don't know what that means."

"It means pretty," he surrendered, and shot Emma a look when he heard her muffled laugh.

The attention of the little girls made him feel awkward. Mona said to him, softly, "My husband, Tim junior, is in the Canadian Forces. The girls seem to crave male attention. I'm sorry."

Ryder was sorry he'd made his discomfort that visible. He was glad he was leaving as soon as the driveway was cleared. He was no replacement for a hero. Not even close. "It must be very difficult for you."

She lowered her voice another notch, as Tim senior left the room to check the water pipes. "It's hardest on him. He lost his wife a while back and seems to age a year for every day Tim is gone."

Losses. Ryder had read the elder man's face correctly. This family was handling their own fears and troubles.

"Do you have power at your place?" Ryder

asked, changing the subject. He tried to sound casual. In actual fact, he hoped the fresh-made bread meant the Fenshaw house had power because he would feel better if Emma went there when he left.

"No," Mona said. "I have a great old wood-burning stove, the kind the pioneers had. You can cook on it, it has an oven. It's fantastic. It heats the whole house, though the house isn't as large as this one."

Again, there was the sense of *needing* to go, the momentary helpless frustration, and then surrender.

He wasn't going anywhere until they got the driveway cleared. He might as well enjoy the mouthwatering bread, the homemade jams, the hot coffee. He might as well enjoy the innocence of those children, the fact that they liked him without any evidence that they should.

"Would you like to hold Bebo?" Peggy asked him.

He heard Emma laugh again as he tried to think of a diplomatic response, and then she rescued him by saying, "I'd like to hold her, Peggy."

"*Me,*" Tess yelled, and Peggy surrendered

her doll to the baby even though Tess was covered in jam.

Of course, surrendering to enjoyment was like surrendering to the magic that was wrapping itself around him, trying to creep inside him. Somehow as he filled up on breakfast and giggles, he became aware something was changing. He felt not *trapped,* somehow. Not ecstatic, either, but not trapped.

"Water's fine so far. What do you think we start clearing first?" Tim asked Emma, coming back into the room. "Pond or driveway?"

"Driveway," Emma said.

And Ryder might have appreciated how practical she was being—since no one could even get to the pond without the driveway, except that she looked right at him, and smiled sunnily. "Mr. Richardson is anxious to go." She didn't say it, but she might as well have, *And we're anxious to have him leave.*

He felt stung. Because for some reason he had thought she was anxious to have him stay. But she wouldn't look at him, and he remembered he had seen heartbreak in her devotion to this house.

His leaving was what was best for everyone,

some sizzle in the air between him and Emma was not going to pass if it was tested by too much time together.

"Let's see what I remember about using a chain saw," Ryder said, and got up when Tim moved to the door.

At the door he saw the older man pause, smile at the commotion. "Look at them girls with that baby. It's like Christmas came early for them."

Ryder looked back, and his heart felt as though a fist was squeezing it. Tess waddled back and forth between the two girls, Peggy's doll in a grubby death grip. The girls clapped and encouraged her every step.

The sense of his own inadequacy, from which he had taken a quick break, languishing in the warmth of Emma's approval, came back with a vengeance.

Ryder felt, acutely, the thing he could not give Tess.

This.

Family. She needed the thing he was most determined not to leave himself open to ever again.

He wondered if Emma was right about there being only one right decision, or if only the most selfish of men would think he could possibly know what was best for that baby, think that he could give her everything she needed.

Not because it was what was best for her. But because he loved her. Hopelessly and helplessly and she was all that was left of his world.

Tess normally kept a sharp eye out for any indication of a good-bye. When he left for work in the mornings, she would arch herself over Mrs. Markle's arms in a fit of fury. But this morning, covered in jam from her fingers to her ears, she did not seem to notice he was preparing to leave her in the care of strangers.

He was relieved that she was not making a fuss about the fireplace, either, though every now and then she would cast it a wary look, then look to the girls to see if they noticed the fire-breathing monster in the room with them.

It wasn't really as if he was leaving her with strangers. Somehow in one night Emma was not a stranger, and he seriously doubted the Fenshaws remained strangers to anyone for more than a few seconds.

He turned away from the play of the children and went out to his car to retrieve the boots and gloves he had packed for the cottage because

Tess loved to play in the snow. He didn't even go back in to put them on, refusing to subject himself to the warmth of that scene again. He slid his winter clothes over what he was wearing.

Tim put him to work straight away.

Two huge trees and several smaller ones had fallen over the driveway. Branches littered the entire length of the road.

Ryder soon found himself immersed in the work of cutting the trees, bucking the branches off them. The pure physical activity soothed something in him, much like the punishing workouts he did at the gym.

Plus, working with a chain saw was tricky and dangerous. There was no room for wandering thoughts while working with a piece of equipment that could take off a limb before you blinked.

Out of the corner of his eye, he saw Emma leave the house and come down the driveway to join them.

"They kicked me out. Mona said I can't even be trusted in a kitchen with full power, but I think the truth is they wanted the baby to themselves. Pigeon convention in full swing."

It was only a mark of how necessary it was that

he leave that he appreciated how carefully she had listened to him last night.

"Oh, and I buried the hot dogs in a snowdrift outside the back door."

Emma was dressed casually, in a down parka, her crazy hair sticking out from under a red toque. She had on men's work gloves that made her hands look huge at the ends of her dainty wrists.

"Tess okay with you leaving?" he asked her, idling the chain saw, worried that the incident with the fire could be repeated now that both he and Emma had left the house.

But Emma reassured him. "Tess appears to be having the time of her life. They've heated up some water. Mona is showing Sue and Peggy how to bathe a baby. They're using a huge roasting pan for a tub, in front of the fire. I nearly cooed myself it was so darned cute. I told them to take some pictures for you. I can e-mail them to you. After."

After. After he was gone. Setting up a little thread of contact, making his leaving not nearly as complete as he wanted to make it. He wanted to leave this place—and all the uncomfortable feelings it had conjured up—and not look back.

"Watch for the ice," he told her, not wanting to encourage her to send him pictures. "Every now and then it breaks off the wires or the trees and falls down like a pane of glass."

"You watch out, too," she said.

"For?"

She scooped up a handful of snow, balled it carefully, hurled it at his head. It missed and hit him square in the chest.

Don't do it, he ordered himself. Despite her acting as if she was as eager for him to leave as he was to go, she was looking for that hole in his defenses again. Intentionally or not?

Despite his strict order to himself, he set down the chain saw, idling, scooped up a handful of snow, formed it into a solid ball. She was already running down the driveway, laughing, thinking she'd escaped.

He let fly the snowball. It missed. And for a moment, without thought, without any kind of premeditation, without analysis, he was his old self again, just an ordinary guy who couldn't stand the fact he'd missed. He scooped up another handful of snow, went down the driveway after her. She laughed and scooted off the road, ducked behind a tree. His snowball splatted against it.

"Na, na," she said. She peeked out and flagged her nose at him.

He let fly again, she ducked behind the tree. Splat. He scooped snow, moved in closer, she darted to another tree. A snowball flew out from behind it, and hit him squarely in the face.

It was a damned challenge to his manhood! He wiped the snow away and made ammunition. When she showed herself again, he let fly with one snowball after another, machine-gun-like. He thought she'd run, or better, beg for mercy, but she didn't. She grabbed an armload of snow, ran right into the hail of his fire and jammed the white fluffy stuff right down his pants!

He burst out laughing. "You know how to put out a fire, don't you, Emma?"

"Were you on fire?" she asked, all innocence.

No. Not yet. But if he was around this kind of temptation much longer he was going to be.

He shook his head, moved away from her, ordered himself again to stop it. But he didn't. "Watch your back," he warned her.

But she just laughed, moved past him down the

driveway. He went back to his chain saw, still idling, and stopped for a moment to watch her pulling branches off the road, blowing out puffs of wintry air as she applied herself to the task.

He frowned. She was tackling branches way too big for her.

"Save your breath," Tim said, following his gaze. "If you tell her it's a man's work she'll be trying to find her own chain saw. Stubborn as a mule."

But he said it with clear affection.

"It runs in her family." That was said without so much affection.

Don't ask, Ryder said. He hoped to begin the process of disengaging himself, but somehow he had to ask.

"What's her family like?"

"There's just her and her mother now that her grandmother died." He hesitated, stared hard at Ryder, weighing something. "Lynelle ain't gonna be takin' home the Mama of the Year award."

"But she's coming for Christmas, right?" Why did he care? Why did it feel as if it relieved him of some responsibility? He had to get out of here. He was not responsible for Emma's happiness. How could he be? He couldn't even be responsible for his own anymore. He was broken. Broken people couldn't fix things, they could only make them worse.

"Humph," Tim said crankily, "Emma's mother, Lynelle, doesn't give a lick about this place, never will."

"It's not about the place," Ryder said, aggrieved. "It's about her daughter."

Tim looked troubled, and Ryder could clearly see in his face he wasn't sure if Lynelle gave a lick about her daughter, either, though he stopped short of saying that.

"Ah, well," Tim said. "You can't choose your family."

Since Tim clearly didn't feel that way about his own family, it was a ringing indictment of Emma's. Ryder had fished for more information about Emma, but now he was sorry for what he'd found out. She was as alone as he was. Maybe more so. She didn't have Tess.

Tim's revelations made Ryder see Emma's need to make a perfect Christmas in a new light. It was as if she thought that if she could create enough festive atmosphere, help enough people, she could outrun her own pain and loneliness.

In a way, he and Emma were doing the very opposite things to achieve the same result.

Troubled, he focused on the tasks at hand, but despite working steadily they had made almost no headway on the driveway by noon. A bell rang, and Ryder realized Mona was calling them for lunch, and that he was famished.

"Mama!" Tess crowed when she saw him. She was seated in her high chair in front of the fire, both little girls standing on chairs beside her, patiently working combs and gentle fingers through Tess's wet hair. She had obviously had a bath, been dressed in fresh onesies from her baby bag, and was proudly sporting a pure white Christmas bow in the center of her chest.

Emma came in behind him stomping snow off her boots.

"Isn't that cute?" she asked. "She looks like a pint-sized queen commanding her attendants."

He kicked off his own boots, walked in and inspected Tess's 'do. The worst of the tangles were out of her hair. Experimentally, he reached out and touched.

Tess screeched.

The older girl said sternly, "Tess, that is enough of that!"

And Tess stopped, just like that. He touched her hair again, and the baby gave her captors a sly look and made a decision. She cooed, "Mama."

"He's not your mama, silly," the older girl, Sue, said again. "Papa."

"I'm her uncle."

"Uncle," the child said, not missing a beat, pointing at him. "That's your uncle, Tess."

"Ubba."

Three months he'd been trying to coax his niece to call him anything but Mama.

And he hadn't been able to.

Girls, women, knew these things. They knew by some deep instinct how to deal with babies. How to raise children. What did he know of these things? How could he ever do this job justice?

Really, in the end he just wanted to know he was doing a good enough job, and for one moment Emma had made him feel that way. Made him feel that he didn't have to be an exquisite baby hairdresser, or nominated for guardian of the year.

In Emma's eyes in that moment this morning

when he had rescued Tess from her fire-breathing dragon, he had felt certainty. His love for the baby was enough.

Or was it? What about moments such as these that his brokenness, his unwillingness to reengage in the risky business of loving others would deprive Tess of?

And he wondered, even if he never gave Emma his e-mail address, just how completely he was going to be able to leave this behind.

Peggy, the smaller of the girls, approached him while they ate.

"Would you like to see my drawing?"

"Uh, okay."

She handed it to him. A little blobby baby, obviously Tess because of the hair, smiled brightly in front of a Christmas tree.

"That's very nice," he said awkwardly. "I like the way you did Tess."

"It's before we fixed her hair." Peggy beamed at him as if he had handed her a golden wand that granted wishes. As if he was *enough.*

Then he had to admire Sue's drawing, too. Sue had drawn a picture of a man in a uniform in front of a Christmas tree.

"That's my dad," she said.

Something about the way she said it—so proud, so certain her dad could make everything right in her world—made him ache for the moment he had not made right and could never bring back. It made him ache for the moments of fatherhood his brother was never going to have, for the moments Tess was never going to have. His sorrow fell over the moment like a dark cape being thrown over light.

It was light that Emma, with her innate sense of playfulness, her ability to sneak by his defenses with falling mattresses and flying snowballs was bringing to his world.

He got up quickly, without looking at Emma, went outside and back to the soothing balm of hard, physical, mind-engaging labor.

"No Holiday Happenings again tonight," Emma said, as they finally reached the base of her driveway. They had spent the whole afternoon clearing it. It was now late in the day, the sun low in the sky, a chill creeping back into the air.

She was so aware of Ryder, the pure physical presence of the man, as he stood beside her surveying her driveway where it intersected with the main road. The sun had been shining brilliantly up until a few minutes ago, and he had stripped down to his T-shirt. His arm muscles were taut and pumped from the demands of running that chain saw. She could smell something coming off him, enticing, as crystal-clear and clean as the ice falling off the tree branches and telephone wires.

From the way he'd been dressed when he arrived last night, she had assumed he was a high-powered professional, and he had confirmed that when he had told her he was an architect. But seeing him tackle the mess in her driveway, his strength unflagging, hour after grueling hour, she had been awed by the pure masculine power of the man.

The way he worked told her a whole lot more about him than his job description. Even Tim, whose admiration was hard-won, had looked over at Ryder working and when Emma went by with a load of branches, had embarrassed her by saying, a little too loudly, "That one's a keeper."

So she'd said just as loudly, "And what would *you* keep him for?" But then she'd been sorry, because Tim missed his son, and could have used another man around to help him with his own place, never mind all that he had taken on at hers.

Ryder was leaving as soon as he could. And that was wise. She realized he was right to want to leave. She realized it was in her best interests for him to go. Something was stirring in her that she thought she had put away in a box marked Childish Dreams and Illusions after the devastation of Peter's fickleness.

Now she stared up the main road. It was as littered with debris, broken boughs and fallen trees as her driveway had been. In the far distance, she listened for the sounds of rescue, chain saws or heavy equipment running, but she heard absolutely nothing.

"I guess Tess and I aren't going anywhere today," Ryder said.

She cast a look at his face. He looked resigned, like a soldier who had just been told he had more battles to fight. It wasn't very flattering.

But the way his gaze went to her lips was, except that he took a deep breath and moved away from her.

Emma watched him go, and despite the fact

she was exhausted after the hard day of physical labor, she felt a little tingle of pure awareness that made her feel alive, and as though her life was full of possibilities.

Stop it, she ordered herself. *Be despondent! No Holiday Happenings for the second night in a row? And the road closed. For how long?* She needed to get that bus ticket to her mother.

It was a disaster! A harbinger of another Christmas disaster.

And yet, despite the fact this year was shaping up about the same way, the road to her inn obviously impassable, something inside her was singing! And it wasn't wild-child, either, though she had definitely perked up at the way Ryder had looked at her lips moments ago.

No, it was another part of her, singing because of flying snowballs and the way he had looked so awkward and adorable studying the girls' drawings.

The rational part of her knew that saying goodbye would be the best thing, but how quickly her own life—Holiday Happenings, even her Christmas-day celebrations—were taking a backseat to rationality.

That was her weakness, and it ran in the family. After watching her mother toss her life to the wind every time a new and exciting man blew in, Emma had done the very same thing with Peter! She had tried to make herself over in the image Peter Henderson had approved of.

She had been amazed when Peter—wealthy, handsome, educated, sophisticated—a doctor and her boss, had asked her out. To her, he had been everything she dreamed of—stable, successful, *normal,* from a stellar family.

Only, it hadn't been very long before she discovered that keeping up with appearances, which, admittedly, had impressed her at first, was an obsession with him. His shoes had to be a certain make, his ties were imported, his teeth were whitened. Looking good, no matter how he was feeling on the inside, was a full-time job for him.

And it hadn't taken very long for him to turn his critical eye on her. *You're not going to wear that are you?* Or *It would have been better, when you met Mrs. Smith, if you said you enjoyed your Christmas charity work instead of telling her that dreadful story about the homeless man.*

And Emma had gone overboard trying to

please him, worn herself out, lived for the praise and approval that never came.

Despite his pedigree, it had all started to remind her a little bit of her relationship with her mother: she was looking for things the other person never intended to give her.

The truth was that she'd been glad when her grandmother had needed her, glad that she had a place to go, glad to escape from the demands of the role she had to play for him.

When she'd finally invited Peter to White Pond Inn, halfway through the renovation, thinking he would love it and see what a beautiful summer place it could make for them once they were married, he had hated it. He had told her, snobbishly, with *hostility*, that she was trying to make a silk purse out of a sow's ear.

That was something else he had in common with her mother, who hated this place so much she hadn't even come back for Granny's funeral.

And then the final blow—by telephone, the coward! Monique was more suited to his world. It was Emma's own fault for going to the inn. For putting her interests ahead of his.

How had the love of her life, the man who was

her dream, turned out to be a snobby version of her mother? To both of them, their interests came first. They didn't even hesitate to divest themselves of anyone or anything that asked something of them, that wanted a return on an investment. And Emma had bought into it for so long, telling herself real love didn't ask for anything. It only gave, never took, exhausting and unrewarding as that was.

Why did Emma think Lynelle would come for Christmas when she hadn't even come to her own mother's funeral?

She'll come, Emma told herself. *She said she would come.* But a promise in her mother's world was not always something you could take to the bank. The doubt was going to be there until the moment her mother stepped off the bus.

And Emma felt guilty about her lack of faith in Lynelle.

"Emma, Emma, Emma," her mother had said, annoyed, the last time they'd spoken and Emma had pressed for an answer about Christmas. "Where *do* you get that sentimental streak from?"

As if somehow Emma was in the wrong for wanting her to come.

"Okay, okay, *okay,*" Lynelle had finally said, irritated. "I'll come. Send the damned ticket. Are you happy now?"

"Hey," Ryder said. When had he come back beside her? "Don't take it like that. The road could be open tonight." And then, softer, "Please don't cry."

Which was when she realized she was crying! She swiped at her cheeks with a mittened hand. "I'm not crying," she said stubbornly. "I poked myself in the eye with a branch."

She held out a branch to show him, but he looked right past it and right past the words.

He cupped her chin in his gloved hand, slipped the glove off his other hand with his teeth, brushed the tear from her cheek. She saw the struggle in his face, knew he wanted nothing more than to walk away from her pain.

And she knew she was seeing something he tried to hide when he didn't walk away, or couldn't.

"Come on," he said, throwing a casual brotherly arm over her shoulder, guiding her away from the road, "you'll have a good Christmas this year. Meanwhile, let's see what that miracle worker Mona has planned for supper."

As soon as he walked in the door, Sue and Peggy, who had apparently lugged Tess around all afternoon, were on him as if he were a favored uncle. They handed over Tess, who now sported several more bows, somewhat reluctantly.

"Mama," she said.

"No, Tess," Sue said sternly.

"Ubba?" Tess guessed.

"Yes!" The gleeful girls danced around as if Tess had scored a touchdown. Ryder stroked Tess's combed hair, and Tess didn't even howl a protest.

"Me preffree," she declared to her uncle. "Har."

"She means she's pretty," Sue translated officiously. "'Cause of her hair."

"Pretty," Ryder said thoughtfully. "No, I don't think so."

All three girls looked shattered at his pronouncement, but the smiles started when he said, "Um, no, pretty isn't good enough. Lovely?" He seemed to think it over, regarded Tess, then shook his head. "Gorgeous. Beautiful. Stunning. Dazzling."

"Creative!" Sue crowed, and he smiled.

And then he lifted his niece up with that easy masculine grace, dangled her over his head, her little legs waggling with glee, and then he swooped her down and blew a kiss onto her belly.

Emma could have watched him play with the baby forever. But even thinking that word in close proximity to him seemed to be inviting danger, so she deliberately turned her back on the scene and went in search of Mona. Mona was on the back porch, assembling the bundles of balsam and fir and spruce that went into wreaths.

"The road's not open," Emma said, glad to have this moment alone with Mona. "I'm not sure we need any more of those. We probably won't be able to sell what we have."

She took a deep breath, "I appreciate you and Tim and the girls spending the day, but I'm not sure about tomorrow. If Holiday Happenings doesn't happen soon, I'm not going to be able to pay you."

Mona gave her an insulted look. "We came as your neighbors and your friends today, not as your employees, and we'll be here as long as you need us."

Emma could feel those awful tears burning in her eyes again.

"Besides, you know how I love this house and it's good to keep busy. It keeps all of us from thinking about Tim. Two more Canadian soldiers were wounded yesterday."

And then Mona's eyes were full of tears, too, but she quickly brushed them aside. "Let's have supper at my place. I can cook on the wood burner. I took out chicken this morning. Plus the whole house will be nice and warm from the woodstove."

The thought of so much warmth—physical and emotional—was more than Emma could refuse.

But Ryder refused with ease, closing something in himself that had opened during the snowball fight. "Tess and I will stay here," he said. "I've got food for her. I can have a hot dog for supper."

Emma knew something about all this bothered him: the children, the family, the moments of playfulness, the togetherness. She could see that he deliberately planned to turn his back on it. She refused to beg him to come, which woman-scorned was very pleased about. Emma knew he was posing a danger to her. She could see that by coming to the inn she had deliberately removed herself from all those things that, after Peter, she was ill-equipped to handle.

But Mona was having none of it. "You are not having a hot dog for supper after the kind of work you did today."

Ryder still looked stubborn.

Peggy came and took his hand, shook it vigorously to make sure she had his full attention. "Tess *has* to come to my house. I want to show her my dollhouse that my daddy made."

"I could use another man," Tim said, clearly having to overcome his pride to ask. "The pump won't be working, and I'll need to haul water from the creek."

Emma was not sure which of those arguments won him over, but she was aware of the sweet sensation within herself of *wanting* to be with him and to spend more time with him, and being glad she didn't have to reveal any of that by convincing him herself.

Somehow they all managed it in one trip, Mona on the snowmobile behind her father-in-law, Ryder, Emma, girls and baby squashed onto the sled.

Ryder went in first, Emma between his legs, the baby on her lap. She had to push hard into his chest to make room for Sue and Peggy, who squeezed in practically on top of her and the baby.

The extremely crowded ride the short distance to the Fenshaws' should have been uncomfortable. Instead, it felt incredible. It wasn't just because she was so close to him, though she could feel his heart beating through his jacket, feel the steel of his strong legs where they formed a V around the small of her back. It was the whole picture, the baby and the girls shouting with laughter as their grandfather picked up speed, the snowmobile cutting a smooth path through the snow.

It was the party atmosphere the Fenshaws insisted on creating, as if closed roads and downed power lines were exactly the excuse they'd been looking for to spend some time together.

It was the feeling of family that Emma had yearned for her entire life.

The house Mona had come to share with her father-in-law when her husband was away was as old as Emma's but more rustic. Inside was as humble as out; it was a true farmhouse, more about function than fashion, especially since Tim had lived here on his own after the death of his wife.

Wall art ran to framed school photos of the girls, and a large picture of Tim, Jr., in his military uniform, smiling shyly at the camera.

There was nothing "up-country" about the Christmas decorations, either; they were a happy mishmash of fake silver and gold garlands, a scrawny tree nearly falling over under the weight of pine-cone decorations obviously made by Sue and Peggy, the table centerpiece a skinny Santa Claus made out of a paper towel roll and cotton batten.

And yet, the feeling of Christmas and of family was perfect.

Peter would have hated every single thing about this house, and he would have called the decorations tacky.

But when she slid Ryder a glance to see how he was reacting, she saw him take in the humble home, something reluctant and oddly vulnerable in the dark of his eyes.

How could it be, that just twenty-four hours ago when she had seen him those dark, dark eyes had made her think the devil had come to visit?

Could he have changed that much in twenty-four hours? Or had she?

CHAPTER SIX

EMMA watched with admiration as Mona, unfazed by the lack of electricity, stoked the cookstove, lit coal-oil lanterns, warmed water for washing, set her old coffeepot on the stove and began to get chicken ready to fry in an old cast-iron pan.

The men hauled water, a hard job that left them soaked in their own sweat and the water that sloshed from buckets. When they were done, Mona gave them a scrub basin filled with the warm water, and dry shirts and shooed them into the back porch off the kitchen. She gave Emma a potato peeler and pointed at a mountain of potatoes.

Unfortunately, from where she stood at the table peeling, Emma had a clear view through the open door to the porch. Her mouth went dry as Ryder stripped off his wet shirt. He was one hundred-per-cent-pure man. He had incredibly broad shoulders, his chest was deep and smooth, his pectoral muscles defined, his abdomen a rippled hollow. His pants hung low over the slight rise of his hips.

Emma felt a fire in her belly. Around Peter she had always striven to feel cool and composed. Even their kisses had been stingy and proper.

Nothing could have prepared her for the pure primal feeling she felt now.

How could she be a brand-new woman—totally devoted to her inn and her independent life—with someone like him around?

He's a temporary distraction, she told herself. But did that mean she could look all she wanted? Was it something like those chocolate oranges that came out only at Christmas? You had to give yourself permission to enjoy them while they were around?

Embarrassed by her own hunger and curiosity, Emma forced herself to focus on the potato she was peeling, but she just had to slide him one more little look. Who knew how long before she would see something like this again?

Ryder Richardson was built as if he had been carved out of marble. The male strength and perfection in every hard line of him was absolute.

He took the washcloth, dipped it in the water, soaped it and then ran it along the hard bulge of his forearm, up his arm to the mound of his biceps.

She hoped she hadn't made a noise! Because he looked up, caught her looking and his gaze rested on her, heated, knowing. He continued what he was doing, but he held her gaze while he did it. She looked away first, her face feeling as if it was on fire.

She didn't look up again, scowling with furious concentration at the potato in her hand.

Then he was beside her, filling her senses in yet another way, the soapy scent of him as sensual as silk on naked skin.

"Wow," he said, his voice husky, "not much left of that potato."

Despite her attempt at concentration, despite the fact she had not looked away from that spud for a single second, she had whittled away at it until only a sliver of it remained in her hand.

"You should go check on Tess," she said, throwing that potato in the peeled pile and picking up another, trying to get rid of him. Only he wasn't falling for it.

"I can hear her laughing. She's obviously okay."

He picked up a paring knife, sat on the stool beside her, took off a potato peel in one long coil, his hands amazing on that knife, his movements, despite the strength in those hands, controlled and fine.

It was very easy to imagine hands like those doing things and going places—

"Pay attention," he said, as if he *knew* she was looking at his hands, and thinking totally wicked thoughts about where she would like them to be. "Don't cut yourself."

She glanced at him, saw a teasing smile playing across his face. The scoundrel knew exactly what effect he was having on her!

Probably because he'd had it on about a million women before her.

"Ouch," she said. She'd nicked her finger.

"Tried to tell you," he said smugly. But then he set down his potato and his knife and lifted her hand.

She who had always disdained the word *swoon*

and the kind of woman who would do it—certainly not an independent innkeeper—could feel something in her melt and slide.

"It's nothing," she said, trying to take her hand away.

He held fast. "I'll finish up, if you want to go take care of it."

"I said, it's nothing." Her voice was high and squeaky, and it had an unattractive frantic quality to it. She yanked her hand away, picked up another potato to prove a point, though, at the moment, she was so addled she wasn't quite sure what that point was.

Her hand was *tingling*.

He sighed, exasperated. "You've got to know when to quit, Emma."

That was a problem for her, all right. Because she should quit this right now. She should set down her paring knife and go join the girls and Tess in the other room. She could hear them trying to play cards and keep the cards out of Tess's clutches at the same time.

But good sense did not prevail. She did not quit. Instead she said, boldly, "Maybe I'll let you take care of it for me later."

And when he was silent she glanced at him and saw he was now concentrating furiously on his task.

Whatever was going on was mutual.

Which made a wholesome farm dinner, platters of perfectly browned chicken, wedged potatoes, a simple salad, seem fraught with hidden dangers—the touch of his hand while he passed the salt, his leg brushing hers when he got up to get something that Tess had dropped on the floor.

Ryder's presence, her aching awareness of him, made her feel as awkward as a teenager on her first date, as if she was just learning to chew food and how to use a knife and fork.

"Mona, you cooked," Emma said after dinner. "I'll clean up. You go visit with the girls. Relax."

I need a break from this man, from the intensity I feel around him, from the awareness of his scent and his eyes and the way his chest rises and falls when he breathes.

"I'll help," he said.

Great. Hide the knives.

Why was he doing this? Maybe because he was helpless not to do it, the same as she was?

Maybe because he wanted to be close to her, the temptation of the faint but growing sizzle between them a warmth too hard to walk away from if you were chilled from the inside out?

Emma did not miss the look on Tim's face. Not in the least judgmental as he looked between the two of them, but satisfied somehow.

Alone in the kitchen, Ryder took a tea towel and wiped the dishes she washed.

"Tell me what made Christmas so bad for you," he said.

"Oh, I wish I had never said that. It was silly. A moment, that's all."

A moment of trusting another person with your deepest disappointment.

The truth was the Christmases of her childhood had been chaotic, full of moves, Lynelle's new men, not enough money, too much adult celebration.

And that shadow seemed to have fallen over the Christmases of her adult life, too.

"One year my new puppy had died, another I ended up in the hospital with pneumonia."

And then last year, when she had so been looking forward to her first Christmas with

Peter's parents, practically quivering with expectation, she had been devastated by the reality.

Not that she was going *there* with this man!

"Just normal stuff that happens to everyone," she said. "I'm too sensitive. Everyone says so. Sorry." *Especially my mother. Repeatedly.*

"Emma," his hand was on her shoulder.

There was that *tingling* again.

"You don't have to apologize for being sensitive. The world could use a whole lot more of that. It's people like you who make everything that is beautiful."

Emma stared at him, thinking it was the loveliest thing anyone had ever said to her. If she got nothing else for Christmas, would that be enough?

"Hurry up," Sue said, appearing out of the living room.

Ryder's hand dropped off her shoulder but the tingle stayed.

"Hurry up. We have enough people to play charades. You two and me on one team, Mom and Grandpa and Pegs on the other. Come on!"

Ryder's silence made Emma look at him. She could clearly see some battle in his eyes. He did not want to play charades.

He didn't say, *I don't want to*. He said, "I can't."

Sue stepped across the floor, took his hand and tugged. She looked up at him with enormous eyes. "Pleeease?" she whispered.

His face looked not as if he were deciding whether to play charades, but as if he was a warrior deciding whether to pick up his weapons or lay them down.

In the end he could not refuse Sue, was incapable of hurting her, and Emma had the sensation of seeing who he really was.

"Who gets Tess?" Ryder asked the little girl, only Emma sensed the surrender, and how hard it came to him.

"We're letting her think she's on both teams," Sue whispered solemnly.

Emma had never played charades, family games not being high on her mother's list of priorities, but the girls were experts on the game, and took great pleasure in explaining her responsibilities to her.

After several rounds, Tess fell asleep on the couch. It was Emma's turn. A little nervous, she drew a card from a bowl. *Love Story*. Okay. Who was the joker who had put that in?

She didn't want to try and act out anything

about love with Ryder in the room. And how was she supposed to get that subject across with only her limited acting abilities?

Reluctantly, she made the motion the girls had showed her.

"Movie," Sue and Peggy crowed together, Peggy apparently forgetting whose team she was on.

So far so good. Taking a deep breath, Emma crossed her hands over her heart, smiled, and swayed in what she hoped was a swoon, something she was newly experienced at. She blinked her eyes.

"Giraffe?" Sue said doubtfully.

Ryder snickered. Emma glared at him and drew a large invisible heart with her hands.

"Giraffe that has swallowed something large. Like a potato. Only not one Emma peeled," Ryder suggested.

Everyone seemed to think he was hysterically funny. He was grinning slightly and she saw that once he had been this man: full of mischief and fun. The grin made him look young, made her think how somber he looked most of the time. What had happened to him? Obviously whatever it was made him the worst possible man to feel attracted to. He was wounded. So was she. That was a bad, bad combination.

Despite knowing that, she went from feeling reluctant and awkward to wanting to make him laugh. She threw herself into her performance, going on bended knee before him, clasping her hands in front of her, blinking dreamily.

"A giraffe with eye problems," Ryder said.

"Would you forget the giraffe?" she cried.

"You're not allowed to talk, Emma!" Sue reprimanded her.

"Yeah," Ryder said. "Whoever heard of a giraffe that talks?"

Emma was exasperated that he would get a talking giraffe out of her practically prostrating herself in front of him with love.

Could she fall in love with him? Given time? Luckily they didn't have time. Then again, how much time would you need to fall hopelessly in love with a man like him? And it would be hopeless. The remoteness that never quite left his eyes, not even when he laughed, was warning her off, trying to tell her something.

Still, he'd walked into her life twenty-four hours ago, and his appeal was, unfortunately, outweighing the warning, swaying her against her will. She thought of the exquisite tenderness on his face when he had soothed Tess this morning, when he had said to the baby, *Mama's here.* She thought of his clumsy awkwardness with the girls, of the way he pitched in to help, of the seamless way he had joined in with the Fenshaws and with her. Emma thought of him telling her about his best Christmas, the light that had come on in his face, she thought of him chasing her down the driveway armed with snowballs. Did all this mean that if he stayed another day she would lose her good sense completely?

"Good sense is my middle name," she muttered a reminder to herself.

"You're not allowed to talk!" Sue reminded her, hands on her hips, frowning.

Emma got off up her knees. Naturally she didn't expect Sue to get her acting out love, but he was being deliberately obtuse. Despite the fact that good sense was her middle name, Emma skipped across the living room, a woman obviously in the throes of love, picked an imaginary daisy, tore imaginary petals off it, *he loves me, he loves me not.*

"The Birds," Ryder suggested dryly, though he was obviously enjoying himself at her expense!

She glared at him, blinked again, blew him a kiss, wrapped her arms around herself and hugged, doing her best dreamy look.

"You love him!" Sue crowed.

And Emma felt herself turn bright red. Of course she didn't love him. She barely knew him! And the little she did know did not bode well for loving him. But she thought of the way he'd been unable to refuse Tim's request for help or Sue's plea for him to play the game with them, and she wondered about herself and her strength and the temptations of another twenty-four hours.

Though surely in these circumstances, seeing how people coped with disaster and with life being wrested out of their control, you knew a lot more about them sooner than under normal circumstances.

Emma decided she better move on before she embarrassed herself completely. She motioned that she was doing the second word, pretended to be turning the pages of a book.

"You're reading," Sue guessed. "A book. A story."

Emma clapped her hands, thrilled to have gotten that part over with so fast.

"Love Story," Ryder guessed, and then gave a shout of laughter, as if his own enthusiasm had taken him by surprise.

Emma realized, staring at him, that what she needed to do was not think about the future or project her romantic nature onto it. She needed to remember the past, and how her ability to fill in the blanks had brought her nothing but grief. With Peter. And with her mother.

She needed to remind herself what grief felt like and to know that the unfathomable darkness that swam in the man's eyes promised her more of it.

"I have to go," she said, leaping to her feet, remembering guiltily her *true* love now, her house. "I have to put more wood on the fire at my place or the water will freeze for sure. But Ryder can stay."

"No, I'll go with you."

Something shivered along her spine. "No, it's fine."

"I'm not letting you go over there by yourself."

Emma could tell Tim approved of that. The independent woman in her was strangely silent.

"Let Tess stay the night here then," Mona said, as if it were all settled, "there's no sense waking her up and sending her into the cold."

Ryder hesitated.

"Okay," he said, reluctantly, obviously weighing out what was better for Tess.

Emma was newly taken by his tender protective attitude toward Tess. It probably wasn't good to be heading over there, just the two of them, feeling like this.

So aware. Her shoulder still tingling from where he'd touched it an hour ago! Woman-scorned told her to go home and throw out every one of those romantic movies she'd been collecting. They had obviously filled her head with nonsense.

"There's an extra snowmobile in the shed next to the house," Tim said. "My son's. Take it over."

For a moment, all the laughter was gone from the room, and Emma could feel how much this family wished Tim, Jr., home.

"I'll be over first thing. We can get started on the pond," Tim decided. "We should at least be able to clear a section of it for skating."

"I'll bring breakfast," Mona said.

And then Emma and Ryder were outside, the

moon full and bright above them, the air crystal-cold and clear, the stars sparkling, close enough that she felt she could reach out and put one in her pocket.

Ryder did up his jacket against the brisk breeze that was blowing. "There's something incredibly admirable about those people. Father, husband, son called to war, power out, roads closed, they just handle everything with a certain calm courage. I admire that."

"I think you handle crisis about the same way."

He looked at her. "That's where you're wrong," he said. He went to the shed, got the snowmobile out of it and then mounted it and patted the seat behind him.

She climbed on, trying to keep the dangerous awareness somewhat at bay by grabbing onto the bar behind her.

"Hold on tight."

So she did, wrapping her arms around him, burrowing her cheek into the strong curve of his shoulder. Surrendering.

They surged through the night, her hands wrapped around his belly. He opened up the throttle and she was sucked even closer into him.

The cold air, the glory of the night and him.

She felt exhilarated. Free. As if there had been no moment before this one, and there would be none after. Her senses gave her mind, always too busy, a much-needed rest. Her senses dismissed the caution she was trying desperately to resurrect.

And maybe he felt that way, too. Because of what he said next.

"Do you mind if I take the long way home?" he shouted over the roar of the engine.

She honestly didn't feel that she cared if they ever went home. This felt oddly like home. Being with him. Feeling his warmth and his strength penetrating through his jacket, feeling the play of his muscles as he guided the snowmobile around debris, picked a route that snaked through fallen trees up the ridge behind both her and Tim's places.

The world was a place of sharp and almost mystical contrasts, the cold sting of night air on her cheeks in contrast to his warmth, the beauty of the moon making the broken trees glitter silver, the forest where she had walked many times damaged now and seeming like a place she had never been before, a place that could hold equally promise or destruction.

He stopped at the crest of the ridge and cut the engine. The silver, black and white vista below them was beautifully silent. They could see the dark silhouette of her inn, Tim's place looking brighter with the yellow glow from the oil lamps lighting his windows. Beyond that, they could see Willowbrook.

"You could almost imagine it was the little town of Bethlehem," she said, the town looking so pretty and peaceful.

He snorted but not with the same amount of derision as he would have done so last night.

"The lights are on in the town," he noticed. "They have power there. And look, you can see headlights moving on the road west of it."

It could take days for those things to happen here, but it was still a reminder that this was all temporary, an illusion of sorts, that would come to an end.

He turned and looked back at her, and then he took off the thick snowmobile glove and scraped his thumb across her lip.

She leaned into it, something flashed through his eyes and he moved his hand away, faced forward, put the glove back on.

He shook his head, and his voice was remote. "I think for both our sakes I should take you back to Fenshaws'. I can look after things at your place by myself tonight."

"You go back and stay at Fenshsaws'," she said, thinking *I'm as bad at this as I am at charades.* How could he not understand what she wanted? Or worse, understand exactly what she wanted and reject her?

"You can drop me off," she said stiffly. "The inn is my responsibility and I'm not turning it over to you."

"If you knew how badly I wanted to kiss you right now," he said softly, "you'd go back to Fenshaws'."

She totally forgot that good sense was her middle name.

"Would I?" she challenged him.

"Yeah," he said roughly, "you would."

"I think you're wrong. I think I'd kiss you back."

He sighed, his breath harsh, impatient. "Emma, let's not complicate things."

He was right. He would be a terrible complication in the world she was building for herself.

It was too soon for this. He was being the reasonable one.

But that's not how she acted. Instead, she got off the snowmobile and went around to the front of it, facing him. She leaned into him, took his face in her gloved hands, pulled his face to hers and brushed his lips with her own.

The first time she had seen him, last night, under the mistletoe, she had wondered what his lips would taste like. Now she knew, and they did not disappoint. Like the other contrasts of tonight, his lips were like ice and fire, steel and silk.

For a split second the force of his will was enough to resist her. And then it collapsed, and his lips accepted the invitation of hers, his hand curled behind her neck and pulled her deeper into him.

To Emma, it felt as though the stars fell from the sky, as if the snow around them turned to fire, as if her heart had been bound in chains and broke free of them.

She had a moment of intense clarity, as if she had lived in a fog, and the sun shone through.

It felt as though every experience of her

entire life had led her to this moment, had made her ready for this moment. It felt as if every bad thing and every betrayal had made her deeper and stronger, building her into a woman capable of understanding what she tasted in him. He was not the remoteness in his eyes, nor the coolness in his demeanor. He was not his shields and not his armor. The touch of his lips told her what was behind those things.

He was the man who tackled those endless physical jobs that had to be done as a result of the storm with the inner toughness and fortitude that gave glimpses of the true spirit she had just tasted.

He was the man who said yes to a little girl who wanted him to play charades even though the part of him that guarded his own preservation had wanted to say no.

He was the man who braved the baby department of a store out of a capacity to love that that ran so deep and so true it made her shiver with awe and longing.

He was a man who could make a woman who knew better question what she knew and hope she was wrong.

"Why *not* complicate things?" she whispered against the softness of his lips, amazed at her own imprudence, but so certain of what she had felt, glimpsed, tasted.

His truth.

"Because," he said, his voice hoarse, "I'm not a man who can give anything to anyone. You need to know the whole truth before you decide whether or not to complicate things."

"I don't believe you," she said, because she knew the truth in him that she had just tasted. "I've seen what you give to Tess." She touched her lips to his again, but he turned his face from her.

"Please," he said, his voice hoarse.

"Trust me with the whole truth, Ryder."

Silence.

"Is there someone else?" she asked, shocked at how devastated that possibility made her feel. Of course he had someone else. Look at her history. Look at Peter!

No, look at him! He'd probably met someone in the baby department.

"No, there's no one else."

Relief, pure and exhilarating, shot through her.

"It's something. Not someone."

"You can tell me, Ryder. Trust me."

He was silent for so long, she thought he might not speak, that he would refuse her the gift of his trust, that he would just start the snow machine and go.

He was obviously having some kind of battle with himself. And she was amazed when he lost.

His voice low, he said, "Emma, I can't love anyone, anymore. Not ever again."

She was tempted to say she wasn't asking him to love her. She wanted a kiss on a moonlit night. But there was something about the ravaged look on his face that stopped her. She needed to hear what he had to say.

And more importantly, he needed to tell it, it was a demon that ate him from the inside out.

"You want more than I could ever give you," he said roughly. "You deserve more than I could ever give you."

"How do you know what I want?"

"Don't even try to tell me you're the kind of girl who could ever kiss a man lightly, without knowing exactly where it was going and what happens next."

"I'm not a girl," she said, but her protest sounded half-hearted. "I'm a woman. An independent business woman."

"Don't even try to tell me you aren't the kind of *woman* who dreams of a man and of babies of your own."

"I have my inn," she said. "That's enough for me."

"No, it isn't, Emma. You want a place like that one down there," he nodded toward Fenshaws', "and you want to fill it to the rafters with laughter and love."

"I don't," she said stubbornly, trying to ignore the longing his words caused in her, the pictures that crowded her mind. How quickly a woman like her could put a man like him in the center of each of those pictures.

"If you don't, you should, because that's what you deserve, Emma."

"It's not what I want," she said, trying for a firm note.

"Uh-huh," he said skeptically.

"I gave up on the romantic fantasies," she insisted.

"When?"

She hesitated. "I had a broken engagement last year."

"If you tell me it happened at Christmas, I'm going to believe the curse."

She actually smiled a little, until he said, "I figured as much. A broken heart somewhere in the recent past."

"Excuse me?" How pathetic was that? That she was telegraphing her broken dreams to every stranger who showed up at the door?

"No single woman takes on a place like the inn without having had romance problems."

No, not every stranger, just a man who saw everything. Right from the beginning she had known that about him. And now he saw she was falling for him, even before she'd completely admitted it to herself. And he seemed to be seeing that, too.

It was humiliating. "I did," she said. "I gave up all my romantic illusions. I gave my life to the inn."

"Like a nun giving her life to the church," he said dryly.

"Yes!"

"Except for the kissing part."

She was silent.

He laughed, but it wasn't a pleasant sound. "No, you didn't give up your longings, Emma. You just wanted to. Your dreams shine in your eyes in unguarded moments, like tonight when you were part of that family down there. They will come right back when the right man comes into your life. Was your fiancé a jerk?"

"He was a doctor."

"I didn't ask what he did," Ryder said sharply, "I asked what he *was*. I've met lots of doctors who were jerks and lots of construction workers who weren't."

"Okay," she said, miffed, "he was a pompous, full-of-himself jerk, who thought he could mold a poor girl from the wrong side of the tracks into perfect wife material. And I was supposed to be grateful for it! Of course, when perfect wife material, pre-made, reappeared in his life, he ditched me."

She was astounded she had said that, and astounded by the clarity with which she could suddenly see her relationship with Peter.

"He never saw you at all, did he?" Ryder asked softly. "He missed it all. The determination, the love of life, the mischief, the generosity. Not to mention a not-bad giraffe impression."

"He would have hated every minute of tonight, and especially the undignified giraffe impression. I didn't realize it at first, but he never saw me, he saw what he wanted me to be. He saw that I didn't use my fork correctly, and that I wore white slacks after Labor Day, but that I had the potential to be *fixed*."

"Oh, Emma."

"But at least he never refused to kiss me!" Unsatisfying as that experience had been— Peter's kisses perfunctory and passionless— Ryder didn't have to know!

"I'm going to tell you why I won't kiss you. Not because I don't want to—Lord knows I want to—but because there is a hole in me nothing can fill, Emma. Nothing, not even the sweetness of your kisses."

He took a deep breath, shuddered, closed his eyes and after a very long time he spoke, his voice ragged.

"A year ago," he said, "on Christmas day, my brother died in a fire. His wife Tracy was badly injured, she died three months ago."

It was as if every ounce of beauty had drained from the night, and left only the cold.

"Tess's mom and dad," she breathed, shaken. "Oh, no."

He held up a hand stopping her, stopping her sympathy from touching him.

But he didn't stop her hand from resting on his chest. She could feel he had started to tremble and that made her want to weep.

"I was there. My brother, Drew, asked me to get Tess out. He was going back in for Tracy. Only, somehow, Tracy was already out, and he was in that inferno looking for her. I had gotten Tess out, and I tried to go back for him. Some neighbors held me. They wouldn't let me go."

The trembling had increased under her hand, she pressed harder against his heart.

"I wasn't strong enough," he said, his voice cracking. "I just wasn't strong enough. If I could have shaken them off, I would have gotten him. Or I would have died trying. Either would have been better than what I live with now."

She wanted to tell him how wrong he was, but she bit her lip and pressed her hand harder against the brokenness of his heart, knowing he *needed* to get this out. This absolute fury with himself, the lack of forgiveness, the sense of failure.

"I loved them," he said softly, and she heard that love in the fierce note in his voice. "I loved my brother. He was like the other half of me. We did everything together. And I loved Tracy, the woman he had chosen to be his wife.

"I failed them." The tremble from his heart had moved into his voice. "I failed the people I loved the most. And I failed myself. A long time ago I believed in myself. I believed I focused my physical strength and the strength of my will on what I wanted and it happened.

"Now I know that's not true, it's just a lie people tell themselves."

She said nothing, keeping her hand on his heart, trying to absorb his pain, to take it from him.

But it was so tragically easy to see he could not let it go.

"It took everything I had when they died. Everything. I can't love anybody anymore. Maybe never again. It tore the heart out of my body."

She did not tell him she could feel his heart

beating in his body, strong, just where it was supposed to be.

Finally, the trembling subsided, and she could feel his breath, deep and even. She spoke, softly.

"It took everything except Tess," she said, a statement, not a question. Her heart seemed to swell with warmth when she thought of that, that he had found the strength to come out of his pain enough to get Tess.

"Yes, except Tess."

"I'm so sorry, Ryder." The words seemed fragile, too small for the enormity of his pain. And yet she felt deeply moved and honored that he had told her this, trusted her with it. And she saw so clearly what he could not see. His strength had not failed him at all, he was coming into his strength in ways he refused to recognize.

"Now that you understand," he said, grim, distant, picking up the armor he had laid down in those exquisite moments of absolute trust in her, "I'll take you back to Fenshaws', and I'll look after the inn."

She knew that would be the easiest thing for him, and probably for her, too. He had told her he had nothing to give, and she knew she should believe him.

But it was Christmas.

And if there was one message about Christmas that rose above all the others, holy, it was that one.

The joy in it was not in receiving, but in giving.

That was true of Christmas and of love. He had trusted her with this, and she planned to be worthy of his trust.

And so she said, gently, "No, Ryder, I'm not going back to Fenshaws'."

CHAPTER SEVEN

RYDER frowned at her. He could have sworn she understood. They could not follow the flames of attraction that were burning hot between them. He'd made it clear he had nothing to give her. Nothing.

"Why?" he demanded.

She looked at him and said softly, soothingly, "Because I'm not leaving you alone with this."

Alone. The word hung in the air between them. His truth. He had been alone with this for 354 days.

"Understand me," she said quietly. "I'm not going to talk. I know I cannot do or say anything to change the way you feel, to fix it, but I'm just not leaving you alone with it."

Others had tried to come into his world. He had not allowed it. But no one else had made this promise—that they would not try to fix it, would not try to make him feel better. Just be there.

He wanted to say no to her. To drop her off at the Fenshaws' despite her protests. But she had that mulish look on her face and would probably just walk back across the snow, through the moonlit night.

So that he would not be alone.

And suddenly Ryder realized the thought of not being alone with it, even for one night, eased something in him. He had nothing to give her. But she had something to give him, and he was not strong enough to refuse her gift.

He started the machine, felt her arms wrap around him, her cheek press into the back of his shoulder.

And felt something else, exquisite and warming. *Not alone.*

That feeling was intensified an hour later as they lay in the same room, separated only by air and a few feet of space, the fire throwing its gentle golden light over them, crackling and hissing and spitting.

"That's why the fire bothered Tess this morning," she said, her voice coming out of the darkness, like a touch, like a hand on a shoulder. "Does it bother you? The fire?"

So many things bothered him. Couples in love, children riding on their daddy's shoulders, Christmas. But fire?

"No. What happened at Tracy and Drew's house was a fluke, a short in a Christmas-tree bulb. The tree went up after they'd gone to bed. Their smoke detector had been too sensitive, going off every time they cooked something. Drew disconnected it. He meant to move it to a different location, but he never did."

He wanted to stop, but the new feeling of not being alone wouldn't let him. "One small choice," he said, "seemingly insignificant, and all these lives changed. Forever. If only I could have gone back in there, things could have been so different."

She was silent for so long, he thought she would say nothing. But finally she did.

"But what if the difference was that Tess had been left all alone in the world? What if she hadn't had even you?"

This was a possibility he had never even considered. Not once. And maybe that was part of what happened when you weren't alone anymore. The view became wider. Other possibilities edged into a rigid consciousness that had seen things only one way.

Ryder had imagined he could have pitted his will and his strength against the fire that night and saved them all. But Drew had possessed every bit as much strength and will as he had. And he had failed to save himself.

So, what if they had both failed, both died that night, Tracy struggling for life, Tess ultimately left alone? Left to complete strangers who would never understand that her eyes were the exact same shade of blue that her mother's had been, that that faint cleft in her stubborn chin had come through four generations of Richardsons so far?

And might go on to the next.

Because Tess had survived. And so had he.

"Ryder," she said quietly, "I know it was a terrible night, more terrible than anyone who has not gone through something like that could ever imagine. I know it is hard to see the miracle."

"The miracle?" he said, stunned.

"You survived, and because of you, Tess

survived. Because you saved her, your brother's arrow goes forward into the future. Tess," she said softly, "is the miracle. Tess is the reason it isn't only a day of sorrow."

He felt his throat close as he thought of that. It was as if a light pierced the darkness. This whole year had been so fraught with emotion and hardship, with traps and uphill battles, that he had become focused only on the bad things. They had overwhelmed his world and his thoughts so much that Ryder had not once stopped to contemplate the one good thing— Tess.

Tess, who had coaxed laughter out of him when he had thought he would never laugh again. Tess, who had made him go on when he would have given up long ago. If not for her.

His journey in the darkness had been threatened by the dawn ever since he had arrived here at the White Christmas Inn. The first ray of sunshine—full of hope, and celebration— touched him.

Tess had lived.

"Thank you," he said gruffly to Emma, aware that if you ever allowed yourself to love a woman like her, she would constantly show you things from a different angle. Life could seem like a kinder and gentler place.

"You know what I would like to do?" she said, after a long time. "I would like to take down every single thing in this house that causes you pain. The trees, the mistletoe, the garlands, the wreaths. Everything."

"You weren't going to try and fix it, remember?" He could not help but be touched that she would give up her vision of Christmas to try and give him peace.

"Still…" she said.

He looked over at her to see if the mulish look was on her face, but all he could see was loveliness. The desire to kiss her again was strong, even though he'd sworn off it for the good of them both.

"No, Emma, I think it would be better for me—and Tess—if I tried to see the miracle. If I tried to see things differently. Before I go."

There. The reminder that he was leaving this place. Before he fell in love with Emma.

But he could not deny that something had already happened. He was a different man from the one who had knocked on her door during a storm such a short time ago. He felt something he had not felt for almost a year.

Peace. Because he'd gotten things off his chest? Because he was determined to see things differently?

Or because of the way he was feeling about her?

"I'm leaving," he said again. "As soon as I can." For whose benefit was that tone of voice? Her? Or for him?

She did not protest or try to talk him out of it.

Emma just said, quietly, "Ryder, until you go, I won't leave you alone with it."

He knew she meant it, and he knew he was not going anywhere for a while, that he was still at the mercy of the roads. Despite the fact he knew he should fight it, he could not. Instead, he felt an intensified sense of peace, of being deeply relaxed, fill him, and then he slept like a man who had been in battle and who had finally found a safe place to lay down his head and his weapons. A man who didn't know when the next battle would be, but who appreciated the respite he had been given.

He awoke the next morning to the arrival of the Fenshaws and Tess. Ryder felt deeply rested.

New, somehow, especially when he took Tess into his arms and she gave him a noisy kiss on his cheek.

"Ubba," she said, and then sang, delighted, "Ubba, Ubba, Ubba," clearly celebrating the miracle he had not completely recognized until now.

They had each other.

"Tess, Tess, Tess," he said back, and swung her around until she squealed with laughter. His eyes met Emma's and he felt connected to the whole world. And to her.

And despite the fact he was stranded, he surrendered to the experience, maybe even came to relish it.

Over the next few days Ryder would become aware that telling Emma his darkest secret had consequences he had not anticipated.

He felt lighter for one thing, as if by sharing he had let go of some need to carry it all by himself.

Now that Emma knew completely who he was, he felt understood in a way he had not expected. Accepted for who he was and where he was.

He found himself telling her his history in bits and pieces, about growing up with his brother, the mischief they had gotten into, the gag gifts at Christmas, the competitiveness over girls and sports, how they had helped each other through the deaths of their parents. It was as if he was recovering something he had lost in the fire: all that had been good was coming back to him.

And slowly, Emma opened up to him. Watching her become herself around him was like watching a rosebud open to the sun.

She shared, with humor that belied the hurt, the sense of inadequacy she had grown up with, the secondhand clothes, the Christmases with no trees, her mother's rather careless attitude toward her only child.

Emma had grown up feeling as if she was a mistake, and she shared how it had made her want desperately to do something good enough to be recognized, how, finally, it had made her vulnerable to a false love.

She told him about her failed engagement, her last disastrous Christmas.

"So, there I was, so excited I was wriggling like a puppy as we arrived at Peter's parents' house for Christmas day," she admitted. "I hadn't met them before, and it felt as if I had passed some huge test that I'd been invited for Christmas.

"Honestly, the house was everything I could have hoped for. It was like something off a Christmas card—a long driveway, snow-covered trees decorated in tiny white lights. The house was sparkling with more tiny white lights. Inside was like something out of my best dream of Christmas—poinsettias on every surface, real holly garlands, a floor-to-ceiling Christmas tree, so many parcels underneath it that they filled half the room.

"Everything looked so right," she remembered sadly, "and felt so wrong. As soon as Peter opened the car door for me there were instructions on what to say and how to say it. Don't tell them I got the dress on sale. Don't ask for recipes. Don't ooh and aah over the house as if I was a hick from the country.

"His parents were stuffy. His mother asked me questions about what schools I'd gone to and fished for information about my family. His father didn't even acknowledge it was Christmas and barely seemed to know I was there. He kept leaving the room to check the channel on the television that runs all the up-to-the-minute stock information.

"We opened gifts before dinner. It was awful. Robotic. These people had everything, what did they care about more? His mother looked *aghast* at the brooch I'd gotten her, his father was indifferent to the cigars Peter had recommended I get him, Peter hardly glanced at the electronic picture frame I'd filled with pictures of us.

"And then there were their gifts to me. Peter got me a diamond bracelet. He called it a tennis bracelet, as if anyone would play tennis in something like that! When I saw it, I felt crushed, as if he didn't know me at all. I never wear jewelry, had told him I didn't care for it. I got a very expensive designer bag from his mother and father. Nobody had put any thought into anything. It was like an obligation they'd fulfilled.

"And the worst was yet to come. Dinner. Served by a poor maid, and prepared by a cook. Naturally, I earned the *look* from Peter when I asked why they were working Christmas day. Then, his mother announced, casually, *slyly*, that

Monique had been calling all day hoping to speak to Peter.

"I knew that was his old girlfriend. I'd worked in his office while he was going out with her. She was everything I wasn't. She'd ditched him to go to France.

"And he didn't even try to hide how excited he was that she was back.

"Naturally, when I called him on his excitement later that evening, I was being unsophisticated. I was the hick. He could have friends other than me!

"Maybe it was the pleasure he took in calling me a hick that made going home to my grandmother so irresistible."

"I think you just wanted to get away from him," Ryder deduced, not trying to hide his irritation with Peter. "He would have killed you quietly, one put-down at time. Why did you accept that as long as you did?"

She smiled sadly. "Ah. The great put-down. That's all I've ever known."

And he vowed right then and there that for as long as their time together lasted, put-downs would never be part of the way he communicated with her. He wanted to snatch back every careless word he had said about her dreams and the inn, but instead, he took her hand, kissed the top of it, a gentleman acknowledging a complete lady. "Their loss," he said quietly.

And the way the sun came out in her eyes made him kiss her hand again.

There was no shortage of work while the road remained closed, and the hard work was as amazing an antidote to his pain as Emma. Until the road reopened and the power came on there was more work to do every day than ten men could have handled. It was back-breaking, hand-blistering work, and it was just what he needed. It was what he had tried to achieve with punishing workouts at the gym and never quite succeeded. Not like this. Exhaustion.

Utter and complete.

He crawled onto that mattress at night and slept as he had not slept since the fire.

To add to that, he had a sense of belonging that he had not had since the death of his brother and then his sister-in-law had ripped his own family apart.

Tim, Mona, the girls formed an old-fashioned family unit, their love fluid rather than rigid, the circle of it opening easily to include Ryder and Tess, just as once it must have opened to take in Emma. It was a plain kind of love: not flowers and chocolates, not fancy Christmas gifts, or dramatic declarations.

It was the kind of love where people worked hard toward a common goal, then ate together, laughed over simple board games. It was a love that toted a demanding baby with it everywhere it went, as though there was nothing but joy in that task.

What had really happened when he had told Emma he was broken beyond healing?

It was as if the healing had begun right then.

It was as if he had given Emma permission to love him in a different way—one that did not involve kisses—and that love—steady, compassionate, accepting—was stronger than the kisses could have been. Building a foundation for something else.

But what? Maybe it was as simple as building the foundation for one perfect day.

Was there such a thing as a perfect day?

People thought there was. They tried to find those days on beaches in tropical countries in the winter. They tried to have them on the day they got married. They tried to create that day on Christmas in particular.

Who would ever have thought a perfect day looked like the one he had had on the second day after the storm? By late afternoon, all of them, Mona, the girls, Emma and Ryder had cleared a ton of broken limbs off the pond, Tim pushing it to them with his tractor shovel, clearing snow in preparation for skating. Tess shouted orders from the little sled they all took turns pulling her in.

An army emergency team arrived on snow-mobiles to let them know they were close to having power restored, and the roads would be reopened within twenty-four hours.

Ryder did not miss the stricken look on Emma's face and her quick glance toward him, but he understood perfectly what she felt.

They had built a world here separate from the world out there and their own realities. They had built a family of sorts, one filled with the things people wanted from family and that he suspected Emma had never had: a sense of safety and acceptance.

But when the roads opened and the power was restored, they were all, in their own ways, moving on, leaving this place that necessity had created. The sense of belonging and of meaning was going to be hard to leave.

Especially since Ryder had no idea if he was taking this new sense of peace with him or leaving it here.

"Enough," Mona cried, as the light was fading and she dragged one more branch to the fire. "Enough work!"

Hot dogs rescued from a snow drift appeared and buns, more mugs of hot chocolate were served from the huge canning pot Emma had wrestled from the warming shed down to the side of the pond where they were burning branches.

After he'd eaten enough hot dogs to put even his teenage self to shame, he noticed Mona sorting through the skates she found in the warming shed. "Come on, girls, let's go skating!"

And soon all the Fenshaws, including Tim, were circling the pond, graceful, people who had probably skated since they were Tess's age.

They were taking turns pulling Tess, still, and he could hear her squeals of delight as they picked up speed, as the sled careened around the edges of the pond behind the girls.

And then Ryder noticed Emma putting away things, stirring the hot chocolate, sending the occasional wistful glance toward the frozen pond.

"How come you have so many skates?" Ryder asked. "Are you renting them at Holiday Happenings?"

"No, people are bringing their own. But there will be a few here for people who don't have them or forget. And the kinds of families who are coming to the Christmas Day Dream probably don't have skates. I tried to collect as many different sizes as possible, so everyone can skate."

"Including your size?" he asked, seeing her cast another wistful look at the pond.

"Oh, I don't skate. I've never even tried it."

Wasn't that just Emma to a T? Giving everyone else a gift, but not taking one for herself?

"How is it possible you haven't tried skating?" he asked. "You must be the only Canadian in history who has never skated."

"Ryder," she said, "not everyone had the child-hood you had. My mother didn't have money for skates."

He saw suddenly the opportunity to give Emma a gift, humble as it was. He would teach her the joy of flying across an icy pond on sharp silver blades, give her the heady freedom of it. He would give her something from a childhood she had clearly missed.

He sorted through the skates, found a pair that looked as though they would fit her.

She sat on a bench and put them on, and he sat beside her, lacing up a pair that had looked as though they would fit him.

"No," he said, glancing at her. "You have to lace them really tight." And then he knelt at her feet and did up her skates for her.

Her eyes were shining as he rose and held out his hand to her. She wobbled across the short piece of snow-covered ground from the bench to the pond.

"You are no athlete," he told her fifteen minutes later, putting his hands under her armpits and hauling her up off her rear again, but then he remembered she had heard nothing but negatives about herself all her life. "Though I'm sure you have other sterling qualities."

"Name them," she demanded.

"World's best giraffe imitation."

The laughter in her eyes, true and sweet, the shadows lifting, rewarded him for this gift he was giving her.

"Hard worker," he went on, "passable cleaner-upper of baby puke."

"Stop! I can't learn to skate and laugh at the same time."

"Smart. Funny. Cute. Determined. Brave. Generous. Compassionate. Wise."

"You must stop now. I'm having trouble concentrating."

But he could tell she was pleased. It was time for Emma White to have some fun, even if it was true that she had not an ounce of natural-born talent in the skating department. She walked on the skates, awkwardly, her ankles turned in, her windmilling arms heralding each fall.

"Can you relax?" he asked her.

"Apparently not," she shot back, and then she dissolved into giggles, and the arms windmilled and she fell on her rump again.

He got her up, glanced at the shore of the pond. They had moved all of fifteen yards in as many minutes.

"Watch the girls," he told her sternly. "Watch how they're pushing off on one leg, gliding, then pushing with the other leg."

She pushed tentatively, fell.

"We're going to go," Mona said. The sun had completely gone from the sky, the ice on the pond was striking as it reflected the light of the huge brush fires they had lit around it. "We'll take Tess home again for the night. Brrr, it's getting too cold out here for her."

And then the giggles and shouts and laughter faded as they moved further and further away until Ryder and Emma were completely alone.

He didn't feel cold at all. He felt warmer than he had felt for nearly a year.

"You want to take a break?" he asked Emma. She had to be hurting.

"No."

There it was. That fierce determination that let him know that no matter what, she would be all right. When he left.

The road was going to be open tomorrow.

And knowing that, and that it was his turn to *give* to her, something in him that had held back let go. Enough to tuck his arm around her waist and pull her tight into him.

It was time for her to skate. He thrust off on one leg, and then the other, steadying her, holding her up, not allowing her to fall. There was something so right about holding her up, about lending her his strength, about the way she felt pressed into his side.

"Oh," she breathed, "Ryder, I'm doing it."

She wasn't. Not at first. He was doing it for her. But then he felt the tentative thrust of her leg, and then another.

"Don't let me go." The end of the pond was rushing toward them. "How do I turn? Turn, Ryder!"

And he did, taking her with him, flying across the ice, feeling her growing more confident by the second.

"We're like Jamie Salé and David Pelletier," she cried, naming Canada's most romantic figure-skating duo.

He laughed at her enthusiasm. "This year, White's Pond—2010, Whistler," he said dryly.

"You might have to learn to lace up your own skates, though."

She punched his arm. "I can't believe I'm still on the ground. How can you feel like this without flying? Let me go, Ryder, let me go."

And he did. She took her first tentative strokes by herself.

He watched her moving slowly, and then with growing confidence. At first he called a few instructions to her, but then he let her go completely. She had about as much grace as a baby bear on skates, falling, skidding, picking herself back up almost before she had stopped, then going again, arms akimbo, blades digging into the ice.

And then, just like that, joy filled him. It came without warning, sneaked up on him just as those memories did. Only this time he felt young again, and carefree, like that boy he had once been on his mother and father's backyard rink.

He whooped his delight, thrust hard against the ice, surged forward. He flew down the length of the pond, raced the edges of it, skidded to a halt in a spray of white ice, turned, skated backwards at full speed, crossed his legs one over the other, and then raced around the pond the other way in a huge, swooping circle.

He moved faster than a person without wings or a motor should be able to move, delighted in his strength and the clear cold and the freedom. He delighted in knowing her eyes followed him.

He knew he was showing off for her, did not care what it meant. He raced down the ice to where she stood, swooped by her, snatching her toque off her head, challenging her new skills.

Game as always, Emma took off after him, those curls gone crazy. He teased her unmercifully, skating by her, making loops around her, swooping in close, holding out the hat, and then dashing away as she reached for it.

And then she reached too far, and slammed down hard. She lay on the ice silent and unmoving.

"Emma?"

Nothing. He rushed over to her, knelt at her side. What if he had hurt her? What if he had pushed her too hard? She was brand new to this, and if she was hurt badly there was no place to take her.

They weren't wearing helmets. And she wasn't tough. Her skull could be cracked open. She could be dying. He, of all people, knew how it could be all over in a blink. How you could be laughing about a stuffed marlin or a snatched toque one minute, and the next minute life was changed forever. Over.

Cursing his own foolishness, not just for playing with her, but for letting himself care this much again, he leaned close to her, felt her breath warm on his cheek.

And knew, from the panic that hammered a tattoo at his heart he had come to care about her way, way too much. And he also knew he could not survive another loss. That was why he had built such strong walls around himself.

Because he knew. He could not survive if he lost one more person that he loved.

And, as he contemplated that, her eyes popped open and, with an evil laugh, she reached out and snatched her toque from his hand, slammed it back on her head, and managed to grab his before she clambered to her feet and skittered away, taking advantage of the fact he was completely stunned by the revelation he had just had.

He wanted to be angry at her for frightening him, and for the realization he had just had. But how could you be angry with her when the laughter lit her eyes like that, when her cheeks glowed pink?

"I'm laughing so hard I can barely skate," she shouted at him.

Give yourself to it. One night. To carry these memories deep within you once it's gone. "I hate to break it to you, but you could barely skate before."

"Not true," she said, spreading her arms wide and doing a particularly clumsy stumble down the ice. "Jamie Salé, move over."

"Somehow, I don't think Jamie has anything to worry about!"

He caught her with ease, tugged at her wrist, turning her around to face him on the ice.

Was it that momentary fear that she had been hurt that made him so aware of how he felt?

Not saying a word, for some things were without words, he let the laughter between them fade and the mood between them soften until it glowed as golden as the pond reflecting the firelight.

One night.

"Though if you want to be Jamie, you have to learn how to do this."

And then, he laced one hand with hers and put

the other on the small of her back, pulling her in close to him. He danced with her. He, a hockey player who had never danced on ice in his life, took to it as if he had been born for this moment.

To the music of the crackling bonfire, and blades scraping ice that had turned to liquid gold, he danced with her. Her initial uncertainty faded as she just let him take her, gave herself over to it, surrendered to his lead.

They covered every square inch of that pond, his eyes locked on hers, and hers on his.

And then it was over, the fire dying to embers, the chill of the night penetrating the sense of warmth and contentment they had just shared.

It was time to end it. Not just the dance, either.

He pulled her hard to him, kissed her forehead where her curls had popped out of her toque and whispered to her, "Thank you, Emma."

She looked at him, stricken, and he knew she had heard not *thank you*, not heard *thank you* at all.

Emma had heard what he had really said. That all this was too scary for him. What he had really said was good-bye.

He could see that she wanted the road open tomorrow—indeed, her business needed the road open. And she wanted the road closed, this cozy world kept intact.

The magic had been building every day that road was closed, and it had culminated in this: for a few short days he had felt young again, carefree, as if the world held only good things.

For a while, here at the White Christmas Inn, Ryder had been free from that place of pain he had lived in. At first he'd been free for minutes, and then for whole hours at a time. Today, he had experienced a day that had been nearly perfect, from beginning until end.

Ever since Ryder had told Emma the source of his deepest pain, everything had felt different between them. He had revealed the brokenness of his soul to her. He had done so out of absolute necessity, and he had done so to back both of them off from the attraction they were feeling.

He was not available. As not available as a man who was married. In a way, he was married to his sorrow. It was his constant companion, particularly with all things Christmas reminding him, triggering memories and his overpowering sense of failure.

He had come a long way, but he did not feel he

had come nearly far enough to accept what he saw in her eyes. She was falling in love with him.

He found himself looking at her now, on that skating rink with the firelight dying around them, the way an art lover would look at a painting. With a kind of tender appreciation for who she was and what she did.

When had he stopped hoping for, planning his escape? When had he started dreading the opening of the road, because he was committed to a decision he'd already made?

The decision never to love again.

And, despite that decision, and despite the fact this was good-bye—or maybe because of it—he could not stop himself from tasting her lips one last time, as if he could save something of her, hold it inside himself, a secret source of warmth when he returned to a world of coldness.

She tilted her head back, met him halfway, and his lips touched hers. He was not sure what kind of kiss he intended—sweet farewell, perhaps—but he did not have the kind of control to execute that kind of kiss.

From the instant of contact, when he tasted

her hunger, felt the passion that lurked just below her calm surface, something in him unleashed. The part of him that wanted things he could not have rose up to greet her, urgent and fierce. Instead of having an experience he could save, he found himself having an experience he did not want to end.

Instead of the kiss saying a chaste good-bye, her answering fire consumed him and filled him. His hands tangled in her short hair—he knew a startled *ah* of satisfaction that it felt exactly as he had known it would—and his lips claimed her and branded her, even as hers claimed him and branded him. He found his hand at the back of her neck, pulling her closer, wanting to go deeper, wanting *more*.

Her tongue danced with his lips, the edges of his teeth, tangled with his tongue, and he thought he would melt from the inferno she was creating. It felt as if the ice could be banished, as if he could be alone no more—

He pulled away from her, but it took every ounce of power he had left. His armor, made of steel, had melted like butter before her.

And he didn't want her ever to know that.

"We should go back to the house. I'm going to go start packing my stuff—" His voice was rough with determination that hid his weakness from her. "—tonight, so that Tess and I will be ready to go as soon as the road opens tomorrow." He hoped to slip out quietly, no long-drawn-out good-byes.

"Stay," she said quietly. "Ryder, stay for Christmas."

"Your neediest family?" he said sourly, trying to be what he had been before, a man who could chase others away with his bitterness, trying not to let her see what had just happened to him.

She said nothing.

"I don't need your pity," he said sharply, trying again.

"In case you haven't figured it out by now, I don't pity you," she said just as sharply. "If you can't do this for yourself, do it for Tess."

"No." He kept it short. If he engaged her in discussion she might think she could convince him to stay. "I *have* to go."

Even without the heat of kisses, the ice was melting from around his heart. Deciding to give into her had been his undoing. How could you not care about her?

Despite his every attempt not to, he was falling as in love with Emma White as she was with him.

Ryder Richardson knew that was impossible. He knew that you could not fall in love with someone in such a short period of time.

But he also knew that love was not logical, and that it defied the rules people tried to make around it.

How could this be happening to him? He who knew the exact price of love, he who knew he would be destroyed if he rolled those dice again and lost?

Better not to take a chance at all than to risk so much.

There was Tess to think of, too. How could he ever be what Tess needed if he left himself open to being destroyed by the fires of love again?

He had to go now. While he still had the strength. Before the magic took him completely and did the worst thing of all.

Made him believe.

Just as the letters buried in her wreath had promised that first day.

* * *

The next day, the road opened before it was light out.

Emma listened to the snowplow down on the main road. Ryder had packed up the night before, just as he had said he would.

Now, as Ryder tried to get her ready to go, Tess was having a full-blown melt-down, struggling against the implacable strength of her uncle's arms.

It would serve him right, Emma thought, if she just stepped back and let him deal with it. But she couldn't. She had to try and ease Tess's distress, and that of Sue and Peggy. The Fenshaws had arrived with Tess and their baskets of food and their hearts full of good cheer, just as Ryder was packing the car to leave.

Now they were all in the front doorway of her house, except Tim, who had taken one look at Ryder's packed bags, sent him a look of disgust and stomped off.

"Shh, sweetie," Emma said, trying to get the hat on Tess's head, "please don't. It's going to be all right. Everything will be fine."

In her heart she felt this was patently untrue.

Sue and Peggy were both sobbing quietly, clutching their mother.

"I don't want Tess to go," Peggy cried, a little girl who had already said good-bye to her father this year, and was having trouble with one more good-bye. But it was obvious Ryder and Tess were going. Ryder's face remained impassive and determined.

He took the hat from Emma's hand, stuffed it into his own jacket pocket.

"Let's not drag this out," he suggested, cool and remote, once again the man who had arrived on her doorstep with his devil-dark eyes and wearing his cynicism like a cloak.

He turned and walked out the door and down to his car, the engine already running, the ice and snow scraped off it.

The sad little entourage followed him outside. Tim, who had been standing on the porch, his hands thrust into his pockets, rejoined them, held out his hand.

"Good luck, son," he said quietly, his eyes searching Ryder's face. He seemed to find something there that gave him something to believe in, because he nodded. But he was the only one who found it, because as Ryder and the baby reached the car, Peggy broke away from her mother and thrust Bebo into Tess's hands.

Emma, hanging on by a thread, bit her lip at the act of selfless generosity from one so young.

The screaming stopped for a blessed second, and then started more intensely than before. Tess threw Bebo, previously beloved to her, on the ground, and arched herself over her uncle's arm with such fury that anyone less strong might have been taken off guard and dropped her.

Emma found something to believe, too.

That another Christmas would be ruined. No matter what happened now—if Holiday Happenings had a thousand people a night show up, if the Christmas Day Dream was a complete success, if her mother showed up beaming more love than the Madonna, it felt as if it didn't matter, it couldn't erase this horrible scene and it couldn't even touch the place going cold inside her.

Because he was leaving. And if he was leaving—his heart hard to Tess's shrieks of protest and the heart-wrenching tears of Peggy and Sue— he was not looking back once he left here.

It would be so much easier to accept that if she had not laughed on that mattress with him, held his broken heart under her fingertips on that moonlit night, if she had not given so much of herself into his keeping, if she had not seen his soul last night when they had skated, danced across that golden ice connected to one another, free, joyous.

All that was gone from his face now, as if he regretted what he had allowed himself to feel as much as she had rejoiced in it.

"Good-bye, Emma." With finality.

She wasn't giving him the satisfaction of saying goodbye.

"Thank you for teaching me to skate," she said, instead. It took every ounce of her pride to choke out the words without crying.

And, for a moment, some regret did touch his eyes, but then he turned from her and put the baby in her car seat, ignoring her flailing fists and feet and her cries.

"Tess NOT go."

Sue picked up Bebo off the ground, wiped a smudge of snow tenderly from the triangle nose and then reached in the open door and shoved the doll back into Tess's arms. She stepped back from the car and wailed.

Emma watched in a daze as Ryder shut the door, glanced at Tim, accepted Mona's quick hard hug, and then turned and looked at her.

What did she expect?

Nothing.

Expectations were clearly her problem, the reason she always ended up disappointed by Christmas. And by life. And by men.

He did not even hug her. He had said his good-bye to her last night on that skating rink.

He lifted a finger to his brow, a faint salute, his eyes met hers and he looked quickly away.

No sense thinking she had seen anguish there. No sense at all.

"I hope your mother comes for Christmas," he said, and then his eyes went to Tim, who had taken a sudden interest in scraping the snow away from his feet with the toe of his boot. He frowned.

As if her mother coming for Christmas would absolve Ryder of something.

"She'll be here Christmas Eve. Now that the roads are open, I can send her the bus ticket this afternoon."

He nodded, relieved. She glanced at Tim who was now looking into the far distance, hands in his pockets, rocking on his heels.

Right until the moment his car turned at the bottom of the driveway that he had helped to clear, and then slipped from view, Emma could feel herself holding her breath, hoping and praying he would change his mind.

"Emma," Tim said uncertainly, "I don't think you should get your hopes up about—"

She held up a hand. She didn't want to hear it. *Don't get your hopes up. About Holiday Happenings. About your mother. About him.*

That was her curse.

Not Christmas.

Those damn hopes, always picking themselves up for one last hurrah, even after they'd been dragged through the mud and knocked down and shredded and stomped upon.

Emma turned and walked away from the Fenshaws, her shoulders stiff with pride. It wasn't until she saw the damned Believe letters in the wreath that she closed the door, sagged against it and cried like a child.

CHAPTER EIGHT

"SNOWMAN?" Ryder asked Tess.

She did not look up from Bebo, her new best friend. Ryder had given her the much newer lavender soft-stuffed pony the day they arrived here at the cottage. Why wait for Christmas? He had needed the distraction then.

He now saw it had been a ridiculous effort to win back her affection. The pony lay abandoned under the couch with the pink suede shoes.

He'd given the shoes to her five minutes after the pony hadn't worked, a desperate man. She had kicked them off in a fit of anger and had not looked at them since.

He sighed, watching her. Tess was sitting on the floor, talking soft gibberish to Bebo, sporting monster hair again, refusing to allow him to touch it.

Anyone who thought a baby was willing to forgive and forget didn't know Tess.

They had been at his lakeside cottage long enough that the accusing look should have left her face by now. He had lost track of days, and counted them now on his fingers.

Tomorrow was going to be Christmas Eve.

"Let's go outside and build a snowman," he said again, thinking she might not have heard him the first time. Building snowmen had been her favorite thing at home, before the White Christmas Inn had become part of her reality.

"Tess NOT go." She slammed on the toy piano to make her point. He had also given her the piano in an effort to distract her from her fury with him. It hadn't worked any better than the pony or the shoes. She didn't play with it, but used it as emphatic punctuation to her anger with him. The tone of the piano was awful and reminded him of Emma's doorbell.

He should have fixed that before he left.

Ryder told himself to stop pleading with the child and take charge.

He could bundle her up into her snowsuit, wrestle her boots onto her feet, put her hat on the right way and take her outside, build the snowman, hope to distract her from his treasonous act of removing her from the Fenshaws, from "Eggie and Boo," from Emma and from the White Christmas Inn.

It would take an hour or so out of a day that seemed to be stretching out endlessly, despite the fact the cottage had a forty-two-inch plasma television set and a satellite that got four hundred channels. He had not found one single thing to watch that could hold his attention, and Tess was suddenly not interested in her old favorite cartoons.

What had he ever been thinking when he had thought coming to the cottage would be a refuge?

Over the last few days, Ryder was discovering he hated it here. He had bought the cottage last summer, a place his brother had never been, no memories. A pleasant place in the heat of the summer, with water sports, along with the satellite dish, to add to the distraction quotient.

But there seemed to be no escaping the dreariness in the winter.

The decor and furnishings, which had come with the cottage, were modern and masculine.

The paint was a neutral frosty white, the furniture ran to sleek black leather, the finishes were stainless steel. The art was large abstract canvases, meaningless brush strokes of red. At the time of purchase, it had all looked sophisticated to him, clean and uncluttered.

Not cold and impersonal, a showroom not actually intended for people to live in. Of course, the cold could be because of the endless damp billowing off that lake.

Or from the way he felt inside.

Like a cold-hearted bastard. *Not just selfish, but mean.* Ask Tess. Ask those little girls who had sobbed as he was leaving. He couldn't even look at that rag doll without being filled with self-loathing.

Little Peggy had been able to overcome her own distress enough to think of someone else first, to try and bring comfort.

That final scene filled him with shame.

Looking around the ultra-modern bareness of the cottage, Ryder missed the inn. He missed doorknobs coming off in his hands, and the imperfection of the sloping kitchen floor. He missed the fact that everywhere you looked inside or outside that inn, there was something that needed doing.

Not like here.

Unbelievably, he missed all that Christmas clutter, the hokey cheer of wrapped packages and angels in trees, white poinsettias and red cushions. He missed the way the tree smelled, and he found he especially missed the crackle, the warmth, the coziness of the real fire.

He had a gas version here, throwing up phony-looking blue flames behind a stainless-steel enclosure, not beginning to touch the chill.

He missed getting up in the morning and having that sense of urgency and purpose.

He missed Mona's cooking, and the quiet companionship and wisdom of Tim, he missed the girls fussing over Tess and jostling for position to show him their drawings and tell him their stories.

Who was he kidding? Certainly not the person he wanted to kid the most. He was not even beginning to kid himself.

He missed Emma. He missed her quirky hair and the ever-changing moss-and-mist of her eyes. He missed her laughter and the mulish set of her jaw. He missed her voice, her ability to have fun, the seemingly endless generosity of her heart.

He missed the subtle scent on her skin, and her hand brushing his at unexpected moments, and he could not get the taste of her mouth out of his mind.

He missed how, against all odds, she held onto hope.

Most of all he missed how he had felt. *Not alone.*

Instead of that he had chosen this. A cottage so dreary and cold that he could not seem to warm it up no matter what he did.

Or maybe it was himself he could not warm up.

That time, the night before she had married his brother, when his sister-in-law had said to him with such honesty and affection, "You and Drew are the rarest of finds. Good men," now seemed like one of the things he had lost to the fire.

He did not feel like a good man anymore.

A good man would not have left the White Christmas Inn, putting his selfish need to protect himself above the heartbreak of a shrieking baby and two little girls who had the maturity to know that even when you hurt, you still gave, you still tried to make the world better instead of worse.

A good man would not have left Tim to be the sole man to try and get that place ready for the crowds that would be descending on Holiday Happenings.

And Ryder knew there were crowds, because the only call he'd made since he'd got here was to the PR firm that handled all his company's advertising. He'd had to go and use the pay phone at the Lakeside Grocery and Ice Cream Palace because he'd so stubbornly left his cell phone at home.

Patrick had promised he would call in all his favors to make sure everyone within a day's drive of the inn knew about what was happening there, and knew what the proceeds were going to.

"Wow," Patrick had said before he hung up, "what a great way to shake off the blues from the storm and get back in the Christmas spirit. I'm going to take my wife and kids out. And what would you think if I suggested people arrive with an unwrapped gift for the families that will be spending Christmas with her?"

"Perfect," Ryder had said.

But it didn't feel perfect at all. It didn't take away one bit of the guilt he was experiencing.

Because all Emma had wanted was one

Christmas that felt good, and he had walked away from her.

It wasn't him she wanted, precisely, he tried to tell himself. It was that feeling of family. He thought of his parting words, hoping her mother came for Christmas. As if that absolved him in some way.

Absolved? He didn't owe her anything!

But a good man would have stayed, not protected himself.

"Well, I'm not a good man," he said out loud.

Tess shot him a look that clearly said *You aren't kidding.*

He remembered Tim suddenly not being able to look at him when Emma had said she would be sending the bus ticket that day, that her mother would arrive for Christmas Eve.

He scowled. Tim didn't think Lynelle White was going to come home for Christmas with her daughter. And, after all Emma had confided in him, could Ryder possibly believe Lynelle would show up?

Ryder could barely stand the thought of one more disappointment for Emma. A phone call. He'd just check. That was all.

He wrestled Tess into her coat after all, but not to go and build a snowman. As soon as he tucked her into the car seat, she started to sing happily. Anticipating a return to the inn.

"I'm not going that far," he said grouchily. "I'm just going back to the pay phone. And that will teach me to leave my cell phone at home, too!"

At the Lakeside Grocery, while watching Tess in the car talking happy nonsense to Bebo, he inserted his credit card in the phone. And then he had to sweet-talk a very cranky operator to get her to check every directory in two provinces before he found the name he was looking for. Thankfully, Lynelle still had the last name *White.*

Finally, determined but his fingers numb from the cold, he called the number he had found.

A raspy voice answered.

"May I speak to Lynelle White please?"

No answer at first, but he could hear loud voices in the background.

"And who wants to speak to her?" The voice became cagey, loaded with suspicion. It sounded like there was a party going on. Not the nice kind, with Christmas music and tinkling glasses. The kind where fights broke out and bottles got smashed.

It occurred to him the words were slurred around the edges.

"Is this Lynelle?" he asked.

"Yup." There was the distinct sound of a match being struck, followed by the long slow inhale.

He suddenly wasn't sure what to say. *Go spend Christmas with your daughter. Tell her you're proud of her. Make a fuss over the inn. Make a fuss over her. Help her have that one good Christmas.*

"My name's Ryder Richardson. I—"

He needn't have worried what to say, because Lynelle didn't let him finish. "Look, buddy, whatever you're selling, I don't want it." And then she said a phrase he'd heard on plenty of construction sites and slammed down the phone.

He took the dead receiver from his ear, stared at it for a moment. Then, slowly, Ryder replaced the receiver in the cradle. He knew there was no sense calling back.

He knew why Tim had looked away when Emma had said she would send the ticket. And he knew why Emma had never had a good Christmas.

From that extremely short encounter, he knew everything about Lynelle, Emma's mother, that you could know.

And he knew she wasn't going to anyplace called the White Christmas Inn for the holidays. In all likelihood, a bus ticket cashed in was what the background noise was all about.

A girl from the wrong side of the tracks, Emma had confided in him, telling him about her botched engagement, bowled over by the attentions of a doctor, probably for no more reason than that the doctor *wasn't* from the wrong side of the tracks.

Standing there in the cold outside the phone booth, it became very clear to Ryder that he and Emma had something in common.

They both longed for a Christmas that could never happen.

His hopes destroyed by death.

Hers just plain unrealistic.

But at least he'd known what it was to be surrounded by a family's love at Christmas.

That's what it was all about for Emma, he

realized. All the decorations, all the holiday happenings, all the Christmas Day Dream.

She still hoped.

Despite life giving her all kinds of evidence to the contrary, Emma stubbornly clung to a belief that life was good, people were good, that given enough chances they would eventually do the right thing.

Believe.

And he wondered if he could be the man his sister-in-law had thought he was, a man he had once been. A man who believed, when all was said and done, in himself. It was not the immature belief that he could just use his strength and his will to create the world he wanted, but the deeper belief that when life didn't go his way and didn't give him what he wanted, he could count on himself to be strong enough, and to forgive himself when he wasn't.

If he was such a man, he would go back there, and turn hope into belief, then he would be the man he had once been. Better, maybe. A man worthy of Emma.

But that was one big *if.*

* * *

It was nearly ten o'clock, the night before Christmas Eve. Emma could finally abandon her post by the parking lot where she had been collecting admission and stamping hands.

She hurried to the warming shed, where Mona gave her a frazzled look.

"Emma, could you go to the house and see if there are any more of the chocolate-dipped shortbread cookies in the freezer? I sold out the last of them that we had here. And if you could put a few more of the wreaths out, that would be great."

Emma hiked up to the house, and looked at the long line of cars parked all the way down the driveway. For hours, people had been walking up from the main road, the closest parking, carrying brand-new toys and teddy bears, paying the admission happily.

"Where did you hear about it?" she asked the first family to arrive, the first night Holiday Happenings had finally opened, after they told her they had driven up from Ontario just for this.

"Oh, it's on the radio." And then they'd given her an extra twenty to help with expenses for the Christmas Day Dream. They actually called it by name!

"Lovely idea," the mother had said. "Exactly what I want my kids to know about Christmas." And then, "Would you mind if I peeked around inside the house? We're always looking for these charming little out-of-the-way places to spend a few days in during the summer."

They heard it on the radio? Emma hadn't been able to afford a radio ad. She'd put up some posters and run a few ads in the classified sections of a few New Brunswick papers. Her budget had not allowed for more than that, certainly not for Ontario.

And who was telling them to bring an unwrapped gift for the Christmas Day Dream?

How did they even know about the Christmas Day Dream?

Now, the day before Christmas Eve, they had gone through all four thousand hot dogs and run out to buy more twice. When she checked the freezer, she found there were no chocolate-dipped shortbread cookies left, and there were no wreaths stored on the back porch.

Emma delivered the bad news to the warming

shed, where Mona was being rushed off her feet selling a dwindling supply of crafts and cookies. She had long since given up on selling hot dogs. All the supplies were out with a cup beside them and a sign that said By Donation. The donation cup was overflowing.

My cup is overflowing, Emma said to herself, watching the skaters skim across the pond, hearing the jingle of the horse bells as they pulled the big sled around the torch-lit trail that circled the pond.

But, looking at her pond, it was as if all the skaters disappeared and she could just see two, herself and Ryder.

If her cup was overflowing, why did she feel so empty? This was her dream come true. The fortunes of the White Christmas Inn had been turned around. Her bills were paid. The store-room off the front hall was filled to bursting with toys and gifts.

The chartered bus to bring people for the Christmas Day Dream was paid for, Emma had enough money to get each family a supermarket certificate for a month's worth of groceries after Christmas was over. Three huge turkeys were thawing for the feast, Mona had volunteers making pies.

Holiday Happenings had succeeded beyond her wildest dreams. Tonight a news crew had come from Fredericton, which meant tomorrow, Christmas Eve, could be the inn's biggest night so far.

Her success didn't feel the way she thought it would at all. She felt oddly hollow, empty despite the fact Holiday Happenings had succeeded beyond what she had ever dared to dream for it.

Maybe the truth about all her ruined Christmases was that no matter what happened, they could never meet her expectations.

What she really wanted was not Christmas. Not skaters on ponds and perfect gifts piled high under the tree, not turkey and stuffing and carols sung around a crackling fire.

Maybe what she really wanted was what Christmas had stood for a long time ago, before trees and packages and music and trinkets had all cluttered the message.

Love.

And that was what had eluded her again and again.

After everyone had gone home, Emma wearily climbed the stairs, and went down the hall to her room, feeling so alone.

She hesitated and opened the door to the green room, ready for her mother's arrival tomorrow night on the eight o'clock bus.

Emma went in and sat down on the bed. The little ghost of the girl she used to be came and sat down beside her.

"We're going to have a good Christmas," she promised her. "Finally."

And in the quiet of that moment, without the crush of skaters and the gallons of hot chocolate, she was amazed that she believed it.

Suddenly, she knew that's what it was all about, Holiday Happenings, the Christmas Day Dream—it hadn't been about giving to others, though that's what it looked like from the outside.

Inside herself, Emma knew the truth. It was really all about her. Every single thing she had done, including insisting her mother come, had been about her, about her trying to be good enough, trying to shore up that terribly shaky self-esteem.

She had been trying desperately to create something that never was with all the Christmas hoopla, with taking on the house, with creating that perfect room for her mother. She had been looking to repair what was inside herself by making a perfect picture outside herself.

The only time she had ever felt the magic she wanted from Christmas was on the pond skating with Ryder. It had not been the wild-child who had skated with him. Not the woman-scorned. Not the independent-woman-innkeeper.

It had been Emma. Just Emma. And with that had come a feeling of freedom, of finally being seen and appreciated for who she really was.

And Ryder had still walked away from that. From who she really was. It was devastating. So much worse than Peter's abandonment, because Peter had walked away from a role she played, not who she was. In retrospect, he had done them both a favor, released her from pretense.

That first night Ryder had come, she had told him bravely, proudly even, "Christmas transforms everything. It makes all things magic."

And now she realized something magic *had* happened. It didn't have to do with Christmas, but with love. Falling for Ryder, she had put away the masks and found out who she really was, become who she really was, and even if Ryder had walked away from that, she wasn't going to.

She was going to give herself the gift she had looked for from everyone else. Love. Surprised, for it had come when she least expected it, Emma felt the exquisite sense of peace that she had looked for her entire life.

CHAPTER NINE

RYDER couldn't believe the cars. The parking lot was full. There were cars parked all along the driveway, and halfway to Willowbrook.

"Don't people have better things to do on Christmas Eve?" he asked grouchily, finding a place, finally, to squeeze his car in where he wouldn't have to walk too far carrying Tess to get to the house and the pond.

But he wasn't really grouchy. As soon as he had turned into that driveway he had felt as if he was coming home.

Tess was babbling happily, Bebo held firmly in her clutches. He'd finally realized it wasn't exactly gibberish. It was Boo and Eggie she was talking to. When she said Emma, *Um-uh,* it sounded like *Mama.* She said those three names over and over again, running them together, in a little melody of joy. She was still humming excitedly as they got out of the car, as she strained in his arms, looking.

He went up the front steps. There was a basket on it, with a sign. Admission by Donation. The basket was overflowing.

He wandered through the house, allowed the sensation of homecoming to deepen.

"Um-uh, Boo, Eggie," Tess cried.

But it was obvious the house was empty.

"Burglar heaven," Ryder said out loud. How like Emma to just trust the whole world—her house open, the basket of money on the stairs. "At least she doesn't have a television anyone would want," he said to Tess, heading out the back door.

He followed the Christmas-lit pathway to the pond. Throngs of people skated, swirling in bright patterns over torch-lit ice. The sounds of the laughter and conversation of those gathered around the bonfires drifted up to him.

It was a Christmas-card-pretty scene. Emma must be loving this.

He moved through the crowds at the warming shed, and suddenly Sue and Peggy burst out of a little cluster of people around the bonfire, looking taller on their skates.

"Tess!"

Tess went shy. "Boo, Eggie," she whispered, and then leaned out of his arms, offering Bebo back.

The shyness was momentary.

"DOWN," she ordered, and her best friends each took a hand and patiently walked her down to the ice and her little sled, sitting nearly where they had left it.

Mona, harried inside the warming shed, looked at him, looked again, and then as beautiful a smile as he had ever seen lit her face.

"Isn't this great?" she shouted. "Welcome back."

"It's great," he agreed, but he felt as if he could not wait a moment longer. "Where is Emma?"

"I haven't seen her for awhile. If you do see her, could you tell her I need some more gingerbread? That's about all we have left."

"Will do. The girls have Tess."

"I'll watch out for her."

Ryder focused on the pond. Surely with all the things that needed to be doing, Emma wouldn't be out there skating? He remembered her delight in her newfound skill. Then again, maybe she would be. Maybe, he frowned, she had even found someone to dance with her. But, no, as he searched the throngs, he did not see a familiar red toque with crazy curls protruding around the edges of it.

He did see Tim bringing the big team of horses around the pond, steam coming out their nostrils, poofs of snow exploding around their huge feet. The harness bells jingled. He went to meet him.

Tim pulled up beside him, jumped down, helped each person off the sleigh.

He turned and regarded Ryder not with surprise, but with approval, judging him a man who had done the right thing.

"She's not here," Tim said, not a doubt in his mind what Ryder had come back here for. And it was not Holiday Happenings.

Ryder felt his heart fall. Not here? But where—

"She left for the bus station in Willowbrook. At least an hour ago. The bus was supposed to be in at eight, so she should have been back by now."

Tim's eyes met his, something in them unspoken.

But Ryder heard him loud and clear.

He headed for Willowbrook breaking all speed limits. It seemed as though every residence and business in the tiny hamlet was in competition to have the finest Christmas display. The bus station stood out for its lack of Christmas attire, a gray, squat building with no cheer, inside or out.

Through the front plate-glass window, he saw Emma sitting in a row of hard chairs, the only one in the station except for a clerk behind the counter. The red Santa hat was on the seat beside her.

Seeing her there, so alone and so hopeful despite the fact it was now nearly nine-thirty, Ryder should have been able to tell himself that he had come back for her.

He should have been able to confirm he was a good man after all.

He had come just in time, to help Emma finally know what a good Christmas was.

He'd come back, a choice. Choosing to live, even if it meant risk. Last year, one year ago on Christmas, standing in the ashes of his life, he had made a choice not to live anymore, and to not forgive himself, ever, for what had happened there.

Now, standing here, he was aware of making another choice, this time to live after all. And finally, to forgive himself.

He'd come back here because he had started off on a road to one place ten days ago, and instead he had ended up somewhere else. And by some miracle the place he had ended up had turned out to be exactly where he needed to be, where he was meant to be.

Was it possible that all things, even the things he had no hope of ever understanding, like two people gone too soon, lost too young, could have a meaning if his heart opened to them?

Watching Emma, he was so achingly aware of what she was hoping would come off the next bus.

And while she waited for it to get off that bus, watched the main door, the place the passengers came through into the bus depot, love would do what love did. The unexpected, the unscheduled, love would slip in the side door.

Hadn't it already? Hadn't it come to her in the form of Tim and Mona, and Peggy and Sue?

Hadn't it come to her on a stormy night nine days ago?

Ryder walked through the side door. A man in chains had entered her life nine days ago, but a free man went to join her now.

Emma watched the clock. One more bus at midnight. Chances were remote that her mother was going to be on it. There was no point sitting here, waiting for something that wasn't going to happen. She should really go back to Holiday Happenings, but she didn't feel like it.

It felt like too much chaos and too much noise, and as if the whole world was made of people who cared about each other and had families, except her. Still, she had herself, and all day she had felt a growing appreciation of what that meant.

"Hi," he slipped into the seat beside her.

Without even turning her head, she knew who it was, let his familiar scent fill her senses. She closed her eyes for a moment, breathing him in, then opened them and looked at him. Her heart began to pound when she saw something in his face she had not ever seen before, not even that night they had skated on the pond.

There was some kind of openness in him, she could see tenderness in the darkness of those eyes.

But of course, she could imagine all kinds of things! She had imagined her mother really meant she was coming.

And she had imagined learning to love herself would be enough, though with him sitting beside her it seemed not that it wasn't, but that loving herself was the stepping stone she had been missing in being able to love another.

"What are you doing here?" she asked. It felt as if she would give away the tiny bit of power she had left if she admitted how happy she was to see him.

"I thought we could start again." He took his glove off, held out his hand to her. "I'm Ryder Richardson, dumb jerk."

"How did you know I was here?" She didn't take his hand.

"Tim told me."

"I hope you aren't here because you feel sorry for me," she said stiffly.

"Why would I be sorry for you?"

"Come on, Ryder. Everybody knew she wasn't coming, except me. Hopeless dreamer. Everybody knew I was trying to rewrite history with all of it. None of it, not even Christmas Day Dream, was ever about giving to those other people. It was always about me trying to repair something that can't be repaired. You can't rewrite the past. It's done. You don't get to do it over, no matter how hard you try. I have a new goal now. To love myself in spite of all of it."

It felt as if she had to be very brave to say that.

"Ah."

"Why do you say it like that?"

"Because I think you'll find loving you is the easiest thing in the world. Speaking from experience."

For a moment she couldn't believe he had said that, so he said it again, leaving no room for misinterpretation.

"I love you, Emma."

When she looked in his eyes she saw it was true. He was offering her what she had never had. A shoulder to lean on. But more. Acceptance. Connection. Love.

"You know," he said softly, "right until the

minute I came through those doors, I was convinced I had come back here for you. Now I can clearly see that's not true."

"It's not?"

He shook his head. "I came back for myself, Emma."

"You did?"

"I came back to save myself. I can't change what happened, either. Changing myself into someone untouchable and bitter hasn't changed what happened."

His voice grew unbelievably gentle. "Maybe it's time for both of us to move forward. Instead of trying to fix what's done, we need to build the future, not rebuild the past."

His voice was low. "Emma, I don't want to be lonely anymore. Or bitter. Or closed. That's no way to honor the gift of love my family always gave me. My mom and dad, my brother Drew, my sister-in-law Tracy. I need to be the man they expected me to be when they made up a will that gave me guardianship of Tess.

"I need to be a man," he said softly, "who can show a girl who has never had a good Christmas just what that feels like."

Her tears came then, and he reached out and caught them with his thumb.

And Emma was amazed that she didn't give one hoot what Christmas felt like. Nothing could hold a candle to the way she felt right now. Nothing.

Not even the most perfect Christmas in the whole world.

And maybe it was because she let go of it, that it finally, finally happened.

Christmas became a dream.

With Ryder right beside her, the next morning as the bus pulled up, they welcomed fifty-one guests to the inn.

How shy and awkward those poorly dressed people looked as they got off the bus and looked toward the house.

And how quickly that awkwardness melted away as the unofficial greeting "elves," Tess, Sue and Peggy, rushed forward to meet the children and to shoo them toward the house that smelled of the turkey that had been in the oven since early this morning.

Mona had a hilarious game set up, an ice breaker, that helped everyone meet each other and get to know their names. Then there was buffet breakfast laid out at the dining-room table.

Soon they were all crowded into the great room, plates empty, coffee and cocoa mugs full, the laughter and warmth flowing easily, the children quivering with anticipation at what was under the tree.

Tim handed out gifts until the room was awash with paper and shouts of glee and exhilaration. There were new snow boots and warm jackets, fuzzy pajamas, mittens and hats. There were toys for the young children—dolls and fire trucks—and electronics for the older ones, portable DVD players and personal stereos.

"Not bad goodies for the techno-electro-free zone," Ryder teased her.

After the gifts, there were skating and sleigh rides, and then after naps for the younger ones, a dinner feast fit for kings.

Then they gathered around the fire once again. Strangers just this morning, they were a family now. A family of babies and old people, teenagers and young moms and dads. Mona had more games, and it was nearly midnight as they all began to reboard the bus, the children clutching their favorite toys, packages being loaded into the cargo hold under the bus. There were hugs and expressions of gratitude and tears.

Mona and Tim packed up the girls, and Tess was put to bed in a crib in the green room.

Emma and Ryder were alone in front of the fire.

"I'm exhausted," she told him, stretching out her legs. "And exhilarated. It was better than anything I planned."

He touched her hair, ran his fingers through it.

"You know the weird part?" she said, quietly, "it wasn't really Holiday Happenings. And not even today, as beautiful as it was."

He nodded. "I know, Emma."

"You do?"

"Yeah. It's this, what we're feeling right here, right now, isn't it?"

"That's it exactly," she said. "Exactly. When I stopped *expecting* the world, overlaying reality with my dreams, it was as if I could enjoy it for the very first time."

And that feeling didn't go away because Christmas had, and neither did Ryder. He stayed.

She woke up most mornings with a kink in her neck from falling asleep on him.

And she woke up eager for the next day, to see what love brought.

A touch of hands, a moment stolen to share a hot dog, an afternoon while the Fenshaws kept Tess.

Ryder and Tess left on New Year's Day.

And that was when the romance began in earnest. He sent flowers. He e-mailed. They talked on the phone as late into the night as they had every day since Christmas.

He came for the weekends, but more and more Emma went to the city, aware that she had missed the city and loved it. Sometimes they would take Tess with them as they explored little coffee shops and antique markets, other times they left her with Miss Markle while they went to the theatre, or out for a quiet grown-up dinner.

The passion between them grew until it flared, white-hot. Every touch, every look, a promise.

But it was Ryder who would never let the passion culminate.

"Hey, I have to be an example for Tess. I don't want her to think it's okay to give in without committing."

For Emma's birthday, in the spring, Ryder gave her an engagement ring, and asked her to marry him.

In the summer, at White Pond Inn, they married, a quiet, small outdoor ceremony with the people they cared about most in the world. Tim, Sr., was there, and so was Tim, Jr., in his uniform. Mona and Sue and Peggy had on matching burgundy dresses.

Tess, in a snow-white dress that somehow had a big smudge down the front of it, was supposed to be the flower girl, but she sat down on her way up the grassy aisle beside the pond, and started picking dandelions and couldn't be persuaded there was something more interesting than those little yellow flowers.

And to Emma it didn't matter. She had given up expectations. And perfection.

And yet, when she saw Ryder waiting for her at the end of that aisle, she stepped around Tess and kept going. She didn't once look to see if Lynelle had made it after all.

They were writing their own history now. Beginning today.

And Emma could clearly see that it was not

Christmas that transformed everything; it was love. And it was love that made all things magic.

And that the man waiting for her, with such a tender light in his dark eyes, was all the perfection she ever needed.

EPILOGUE

TWENTY-TWO gallons of hot chocolate.

Ten of mulled wine.

Four hundred and sixty-two painstakingly decorated Christmas cookies.

And it was not going to be nearly enough.

"If you lift that kettle of hot chocolate, I'm throwing you over my shoulder and taking you home," Ryder told Emma, irritated.

"I love it when you're masterful," she said, clearly not seeing how serious the situation was.

"I'm not joking, Emma."

"Ha. As if you could pick me up right now."

"I could," he said threateningly. He still felt this thrill when he looked at her and used the word *wife*. This woman had come into herself so completely it nearly made him dizzy that she had chosen to love him. Emma was sassy, confident, radiant, strong, on fire with her love of life. And of him.

"Okay, okay," she said. "Tim, could you get this hot chocolate for me? Ryder has decided I'm delicate."

Tim, Jr., came over and lifted the pot of warm liquid easily. "You *are* delicate," he told her sternly. "Keep an eye on her, Ryder. I don't trust her as far as I could throw her."

"And that would not be very far," Emma said giving her huge belly a satisfied pat.

The truth was Ryder had tried to talk her out of White Christmas at the inn this year.

The doctor had told them to expect a New Year's baby. What if they got snowed in, like the year they met?

But Emma had gotten that mulish look on her face and he'd known there was no sense arguing with her. He'd call a helicopter if they got snowed in. He had his cell phone with him, just in case.

Besides, there would have been no living with Tess if he had cancelled their yearly Christmas trip to White Pond Inn.

She was four now, a young lady who knew her own mind. He looked for her—Emma had dressed her in neon pink so they could spot her in the crowds. She was down on the pond, in her new skates, shuffling along between Sue and Peggy. This year, their little sister, born about nine months after Tim had returned home from his tour of duty—was in the sled being pulled behind the girls.

"Don't take this the wrong way," Tim said, following Ryder's gaze to the four little girls on the pond, "but I hope that's a boy in there."

"Chauvinist," Emma accused him, but her eyes twinkled with the shine of a woman well-loved.

"Healthy is good enough for me," Ryder said.

He decided, as long as he could keep an eye on Emma and keep her from lifting anything too heavy, it was good to have come to White Pond this year after all.

She had sold the White Pond Inn to Mona and Tim shortly after she'd agreed to marry Ryder. The younger Fenshaws didn't run it as a bed-and-breakfast, the inn was now their family home. But every year they held Holiday Happenings, though Mona, Ryder thought thankfully, had renamed it Home for the Holidays. The Christmas Day Dream event had gotten bigger, and it was called Coming Home for Christmas.

Ryder suspected they kept both activities going mostly for him and Emma.

Because, as the friendship had grown between the two couples, they'd learned about each other's histories and heartbreaks. The Fenshaws knew this was always going to be a hard time of year for Ryder, a good time to stay busy, to give to others.

"You don't have to," he'd said to Emma when she had announced she planned to sell. Tim, Jr., wanted the inn not to run as a bed and breakfast, but to farm, as his father farmed, and his grandfather had farmed before that.

Ryder had not been looking for a brother, just as he had not been looking for love that night a storm had stranded him.

But in Tim he'd been given a brother anyway.

"No," Emma had said firmly, "the house and land need what they have to give. It's falling down and in need of the kind of repairs Tim can give it and I can't. Mona has always loved that house. Tim is home now."

"If you want it, I'll fix it up for you as a wedding present."

"Ryder," she said, smiling at him. "You don't seem to get it. I don't need it anymore. It was like my dreams, falling down and in need of repair. I wanted White Pond to give me a family, and a feeling of belonging. But I have a better dream now, and I know better than to think a house can make you *feel* things."

And the way she looked at him when she said that made him feel, not ten feet tall and bullet-proof, but as if he was enough.

"Mama, Papa, look at me."

Tess's voice rose high over the sounds of the crowd and he and Emma both turned to look.

Tess's pronunciation of Emma had been close to *Mama* all those years ago. And somehow he had become *papa*.

When he showed Tess the pictures of Drew and Tracy, they were Mom and Dad, and he was achingly aware of never wanting to take their place. At the same time he wanted to do a job that would make them so proud of him.

If Tess's level of confidence was any indication, he and Emma were doing just fine.

For a moment, watching Tess strut proudly across the ice, he felt the spirit of it all.

His brother and sister-in-law.

Christmas.

And he believed. He believed that things had a reason.

Once upon a time, he'd been a man trying to outrun Christmas, finding exactly what he needed en route to where he thought he was going, and had not been going there at all.

With each year that passed, Ryder was able to see more clearly that the fire had taken things from him. But it had given him things, too.

It had put him on the road that had led him to Emma. And it had made him a man capable of feeling deeply for others, capable of forgiveness of failings. He was a better man than he had been before, worthy of love.

That made him wonder, sometimes, if he could find meaning in that, of all things, was there meaning in everything? Even in the things his mind, limited and human, could not grasp?

He was an architect, trained to think in terms of mathematical precision. But he knew, as an architect, that there was a place where planning and precision left off and inspiration began. Often inspiration came as the result of a problem that seemed insoluble, a hardship that did not seem as if it could be overcome.

The greatest buildings came from that place.

And maybe the greatest men and women did, too.

Look at Lynelle. How could someone like her produce someone like Emma?

His mother-in-law had chosen not to be a part of their lives at all. She did not come at Christmas; she said she would have come for the wedding if they'd held it anywhere but at White Pond.

But he didn't believe it. She was as indifferent to Tess and the coming baby as she had been to Emma.

But even his fury at that had been distilled by the love he lived in.

When he looked at Emma and saw her compassion for others, he knew it came from all those years when she had tried to win attention and approval from Lynelle that never came.

Emma showed him that good could come from bad, good people from bad parents, good things from bad situations. It was the fire that tempered the steel.

She showed him every day that love was not a destination he had arrived at, but a journey he had embarked upon. It was full of peaks and valleys, challenges and rewards, but most of all, it was stronger than anything else.

Christmas represented that.

It represented all the things that, for awhile, he had lost belief in.

Goodness.

Hope.

Faith.

Light.

"Papa!"

Life.

Suddenly, Emma's hand flew to her belly, and her eyes widened and then met his. She inhaled sharply and deeply.

"The books don't get you ready for how that feels," she marveled. "Do you think we're going to have a Christmas baby, Ryder?"

The calmness in her face, her absolute trust in him made him remember the other belief love had restored—his belief in himself.

A child would be born and he would be enough to welcome another life into this world, enough to accept the responsibility as well as the joy. It was another thing to celebrate during the season, his list of things to celebrate slowly outgrowing his things to grieve.

And wasn't that really what Christmas represented? An evolution of thought, man's belief that everything in the end had a reason, and that everything in the end was for the greater good.

Somewhere in the last years, with Emma and Tess making his good outweigh his bad, Ryder had realized he could surrender. He could trust himself, but know that when his own strength flagged, or was not enough, that was when the real miracle happened.

The truth was that something greater than him ran the show.

Isn't that what Christmas really celebrated?

The birth of a child that would bring a message to the world.

Love is the most powerful.

Love is the thing that cannot be destroyed.

And it went on and on, even after death.

It went on in a little girl down there a flash of neon pink, shouting "Mama! Papa! Watch me."

And it would go on in a new baby, a new life,

a brand-new messenger of the power of love to bring hope and to heal all.

Despite her saying he couldn't possibly lift her, Ryder swept his wife into his arms and headed for the car. "Tim," he called, "she's going into labor."

"Stop it," she insisted. "Ryder, really! I'm too heavy. I can walk. It was only the first pain."

But the thing was, she didn't feel heavy to him at all.

She felt light. And he felt light. And all of it, the skaters on the pond, Tess, the Fenshaw girls, the laughter, the scrape of blades on ice, Tim racing toward them with a look on his face that reminded Ryder of the soldier he had been, all of it suddenly seemed as if it was swirling together, becoming one immense energy.

Ryder realized, suddenly, his heart swelling until he thought it would break, that he really *believed.*

And in that shining second of pure love, his breath, his bone, his life, his whole world, became a reflection of the Light.

0310 Rom LP

MILLS & BOON PUBLISH EIGHT LARGE PRINT TITLES A MONTH. THESE ARE THE EIGHT TITLES FOR APRIL 2010.

ଔ

THE BILLIONAIRE'S BRIDE OF INNOCENCE
Miranda Lee

DANTE: CLAIMING HIS SECRET LOVE-CHILD
Sandra Marton

THE SHEIKH'S IMPATIENT VIRGIN
Kim Lawrence

HIS FORBIDDEN PASSION
Anne Mather

AND THE BRIDE WORE RED
Lucy Gordon

HER DESERT DREAM
Liz Fielding

THEIR CHRISTMAS FAMILY MIRACLE
Caroline Anderson

SNOWBOUND BRIDE-TO-BE
Cara Colter